D1826529

Hell Riders

Sharper Wade rode into a no-name town, stuck in the middle of nowhere. Tired and trail-weary, all he wanted was chow and a bed for the night so that he could move on come morning. He soon discovered this was not to be. He'd entered hell – and hell wasn't long in sending its riders, the Henry gang

The Henry gang was hired by Ben Robson to find the sheriff who had shot his only son. But Jud Henry had other ideas: he'd seen the town, he'd see Ben Robson's ranch and he wanted both

Now Sharper Wade was forced to do battle with the unscrupulous Henry gang, and hot lead soon began to fly. Could just one man defeat the murderous bunch so aptly know as Hell Riders?

Hell Riders

A Sharper Wade Western

JAY D. WEST

A Black Horse Western

Robert Hale Limited
Clerkenwell House
Clerkenwell Green
London EC1R 0HT

Typeset by Derek Doyle & Associates, Liverpool.
Printed and bound in Great Britain by
Antony Rowe Limited, Wiltshire

You know who you are

ABDtherealman, AnnNova, Annosbourne,
edpickford@cw, Lead@rb, Greta381,
DPeters2, Gatsby726, GCMEE, Jinny39415,
Kaz1505, Kipper2205, Le Dazzer, LooLoo4347
and little Aimee, michelle@greenland1,
Moldymoldy, Mantiet oo, PoPStillCrazy,
Quitter99a, SallyN30, S3r3ndipity Sdsec,
SpotBD, Suxice, TigerBaby8888,
Toolfish, Wren12345, and Venus17337

And of course – FrankieBlue!!

Thanks a bunch for a loada larfs, hehe!

ONE

It seemed like a small, quiet, ordinary township; a saloon, livery, café and rooming-house, complete with veranda and upper balcony with the posts showing flaky paint that once could have been white.

Sharper Wade reined in his mount, the animal snorted and pawed at the deep red dust that made up the main street: the only street.

With his Stetson pulled down low, shielding his trail-weary eyes from the relentless sun, and bandanna hanging loosely round his deeply tanned neck, the fine covering of the same red dust made it look as though rider and horse were one. Sharper loosely rested his right hand on the butt of his faithful Colt Peacemaker, and gently eased back the well-oiled hammer without removing the weapon from its holster.

The fading clapboard fronts of the ramshackle wooden buildings stared back blankly as Sharper took in a broad sweep of the town.

Nothing stirred.

A gentle gust of wind headed down the street towards him, the sand began to dance and Sharper closed his eyes to slits in an attempt to protect them from the inevitable invasion.

The wind rushed past and the town fell back to silence once more. Only the gentle throat rumblings of his mount told Sharper he wasn't stone deaf.

Six weeks out on the trail, living on what he could catch, washing whenever he found enough water and hearing only the sounds of nature and his mount's hooves hitting rock and sand, was enough to make any man feel deaf – or mad – or both.

Ears humming in the eerie and unnatural silence that filled them, Sharper's senses felt keen. Not for the first time, his ability to feel the presence of danger before it manifested itself was acute.

Directly ahead, the dull orange-red globe of the sun hit the distant mountains. Slats of light speared across the land; shadows deepened and from the roof of the livery stable something rustled.

King, Sharper's new mount, was edgy; ears flat back on his head, he snorted again.

'Easy boy,' Sharper whispered, as he ran his left hand down the animal's glistening neck, and the animal calmed.

A curl of woodsmoke crept unwillingly from a

distant smoke-stack, tentatively rising into the now still air. Sharper, hand still poised on the butt of his pistol, glanced to his left without moving his head.

A drape swayed gently in the café, as if the occupant or occupants didn't want to be seen.

Sharper raised his head slightly, sniffing in the air; after six weeks without, the smell of ham and eggs or steak would be easy to detect.

He caught nothing except the comforting smell of King's sweat and the familiar aroma of leather from his saddle.

Again a scampering grating sound came from the direction of the livery stable.

Sharper's eyes darted to his right in an attempt to catch a glimpse of whoever was spying him out.

He saw nothing.

Moving King forward, he eased up by a hitching pole and sat stock-still once more.

The batwings to the saloon were closed and, behind them, large wooden doors scarred with years of boot scrapings, stood locked. Dank and dingy gingham drapes adorned windows either side of the doors, but they didn't move and no light showed from within.

In fact, Sharper realized he couldn't see a light showing in any of the dilapidated buildings.

Rubbing the side of King's neck once more, Sharper decided to dismount. If trouble was brewing, he didn't want his animal hit, and, besides, he'd rather be standing on his own two feet than rooted in his saddle like a sitting duck.

Releasing the hammer on his Colt gently, Sharper grabbed the saddle pommel and hitched his right leg slowly over the horse's back, putting all his weight on the left stirrup before swinging slowly and carefully to the ground and facing the seemingly deserted saloon.

Out of the corner of his eye, Sharper caught movement; a fleeting ghost of a vision.

A hat, high up behind the livery façade.

Reaching for his weapon and ready to dive, Sharper waited for more movement.

None came.

Aware he was a stranger in town and not wanting to get off on the wrong foot, Sharper kept his handgun holstered; he wasn't about to start any trouble if he could avoid it.

Decision time: should he just ride on out and find somewhere else to feed and get rid of the trail dust, or hang around a while longer and see what gives?

Sharper reckoned on the latter.

Bringing the reins over King's head, he led the animal to the water trough to the left of the saloon. King turned to face him, then turned to the water – a fine misting of dust clouded the surface and Sharper knew what King was asking.

Keeping his right hand close to his pistol, Sharper sank a gloved left hand into the water and stirred it up. King snorted and sank his head into the trough.

Sharper removed his bandanna and sank it into the water. Then he took off his Stetson and rubbed at his face and the back of his neck. The water was tepid but refreshing to his skin and he already felt a whole lot better.

Leaving the Stetson hanging by the neck-cord down his back, Sharper reached into a vest pocket, brought out a smoke and dragged the vesta across the wooden trough.

After inhaling deeply, Sharper blew out a cloud of blue-tinged smoke and watched as it rose lazily in the air.

The hat again.

Turning slowly to face the livery stable, Sharper inhaled once more, and through the smoke said, 'You stayin' up there all day?'

The words shattered the eerie silence and seemed to bounce right back at him off the building opposite.

Nothing stirred for a few minutes and Sharper waited – he had nothing better to do.

'You best ride on, mister.'

Sharper's grip tightened on the butt of his Colt automatically.

Was he being threatened?

'They'll be here soon. You best move on!' The voice sounded girlish, but it could also have been boyish, Sharper wasn't sure.

'Can't see no sense in ridin' on,' Sharper said in a low, soft voice. 'Only just arrived.'

'Please, mister. You don't wanna stay round

here, not when the boys come in.'

Sharper drew on his cigarette and threw the butt into the sand, grinding it out unnecessarily, before exhaling and raising his head to the roof-line of the livery stable opposite.

'Horse here needs feed and rest, so do I. I ain't fixin' to ride on nowheres until we're both fed and watered.'

Slowly, a shape appeared behind the painted sign that was only just readable: O'CREADY'S.

The body moved further out and still Sharper couldn't tell whether it was male or female. The battered hat that covered the hair, and the clothes – jacket, shirt and denims – would suit either.

'An' what "boys" would these be?' Sharper asked, keeping his gaze directed at the distant hidden eyes of the small figure.

'Don't matter no which-way,' the figure said. 'You don't wanna know.'

Sharper could see that the figure wasn't armed and that released some of the tension, but there could be others.

Taking up the reins once more, Sharper led King to the hitching post and loosely tied him up before continuing.

'I already said, boy,' Sharper took a guess, 'I ain't figurin' on ridin' on nowhere. So you best get used to the idea.'

'I *ain't* no boy!' the figure shouted back indignantly. And before Sharper could reply, the figure whipped off her hat allowing long blonde hair to cascade over her shoulders.

'No, you sure ain't,' Sharper replied, a grin creasing his craggy features.

The figure disappeared only to reappear a few minutes later, running down a boardwalk to one side of the stable.

'An' I reckon you should start considerin' moving on!' the girl said.

Before waiting for a reply, she spun round and stared down the street. In the distance, almost hidden now in deep shadow, riding in from the sun, a dust cloud loomed.

Sharper followed her gaze.

'Them the "boys"?' he asked.

The girl nodded.

'You wanna tell me what's goin' on?'

The girl hesitated: as best she could she took in the stranger's appearance. He didn't look like a cowhand or a bum saddle-tramp. The long range-coat covered most of him, except where it was pulled back to reveal his gun and holster, but she could imagine by the man's gaze and stature and calm appearance that he knew what he was about.

'You a 'slinger, mister?' she asked, her voice showing both fear and awe.

'Nope. I ain't no 'slinger. Why?'

'Well, you best leave then.'

'We speakin' the same lingo?' Sharper said, irritated now by the same repeated request.

'I know *I* am!' Again the voice was indignant,

dismissive.

'I tol' you, an' I'll tell you agen fer the last time of askin'. I ain't leavin. You got that this time?'

'It's your funeral, mister,' the girl replied with a shrug. 'No one's forcin' you to stay.'

'Well that's one thing we agree on. Now, I need my horse, King, fed and watered and rubbed down. That your job?'

'No it most certainly ain't,' the girl replied, almost but not quite stamping a foot.

'Well, you gonna tell me where I can find that there O'Cready?'

'No I ain't'

'Why the hell not?'

''Cos I don't know. Most folks hereabouts got more sense than you and they high-tailed it outa here for a while.'

'Then tell me why?'

'It don't—'

'I'm gonna whup your smart little ass if'n you don't give me some answers pretty damn soon, young lady.'

The girl opened her mouth to say something, then thought better of it.

Folding her arms across her chest, she thought for a few more seconds.

'It's the Henry gang,' she said at last with a look on her face that suggested Sharper should know who they were.

He didn't.

'An' who the hell are they?'

'You gotta be kiddin', mister,' the girl replied.

Sharper pulled on his Stetson and opened the rangecoat to his left side, revealing another gun and holster.

'Thought you said you ain't no 'slinger?'

'I ain't fer hire,' Sharper said through clenched teeth: kid or not, he was beginning to lose patience.

The girl got the message.

'Other side o' that bluff,' she pointed west, 'Ben Robson runs a ranch, the Big B. He had a son,' she stopped.

'*Had*?' Sharper queried.

'We also had a town sheriff. One night, Sam, that's Ben's son, well, I guess he got a little too drunk an' full of hisself. When Casey Malone, the sheriff, tried to get him to leave the saloon and git on home, young Sam got a mite touchy an' started mouthin' off.

'Woulda been OK if'n Sam had been on his own, but he'd come in with a few of the hands, they was gettin' ready for a drive an' I guess they wanted one last night before the trail dust bit 'em.

'Anyhow, Sam was pushed on by his cronies and he drew.'

'I take it then, he got hisself killed?'

'Deader'n a rat in a trough,' she replied. 'Ol' Casey weren't much of a shootist, but he *was* sober. That same night Casey rode out o' town an' we ain't seen him since.'

'So what's this Henry gang gotta do with it?'

Sharper asked.

'Ben Robson didn't take none too kindly to his only son gettin' killed, 'specially after his wife had been killed only a few weeks before.'

'What happened to her?'

'Horse threw her out in the Mojave, her head hit the only rock for miles around.'

'Shit – sorry, ma'am, I don't mean to curse none, but that sure is bad luck. What's this Ben Robson after doin'?'

'He aims to kill everyone 'til we tell him where the sheriff ran off to.'

'Does anyone know?'

'Nope. But that don't matter none to Ben, he don't believe no one.'

Sharper thought awhile: 'How many bin killed so far?'

'None. Today's the day. Ben Robson gave three days to think it over. Most folks left, them that didn't are hidin' someplace.'

'How come you're still here?'

'Casey Malone was my uncle. I ain't got nowhere to go.'

Sharper was used to thinking on his feet. 'Take my horse into the stable. You know how to take a saddle off?'

'I ain't stupid.'

'OK, keep your britches on. Feed him up an' stay low.'

'What you aimin' to do?'

'I don't know yet, but somethin' sure will occur

to me. Now, git!'

'What's your name, mister?' the girl asked.

'Wade, Sharper Wade. What's yours?'

'Sandy. Sandy Cogan.'

'Good to meet you, Sandy, now git.'

The girl crossed the street towards Sharper's horse. Sharper removed his saddle-bags and a Winchester. Holding on to the rifle, he slung the saddle-bags across one shoulder and watched the approaching girl. As she neared, Sharper saw that she wasn't just a *little* girl. Although she was small in height, she had the biggest blue eyes he'd seen in a long time and a face that held an angelic look about it. No sirree, he thought, This ain't no *little* girl.

Without another word, Sandy led King off to the livery stable; the animal sensed he was about to be fed and allowed himself to be led without a fuss.

'You take real good care of him, missy,' Sharper said. 'An' keep low when them riders arrive. OK?'

'OK,' she replied and disappeared into the darkness of the livery stable.

Sharper eyed the town once more. It was small, nothing much to make sense of it being here in the first place.

Stuck on the edge of the desert, he figured it might have been a staging post that just grew; he couldn't see any other reason for the godforsaken place to exist.

Now, as he glanced around, it was for a different reason. He needed to get the lie of the land firmly fixed in his brain. If there was going to be trouble – and it sure looked that way – Sharper needed to know where the safest places were.

The dust-cloud neared. Through the heat haze he could see nothing, not even how many riders there were, but they sure weren't sparing their mounts.

Careful as always, Sharper checked the breech of the Winchester. It was fully loaded. Next, he checked both pistols, they too were loaded, five to each cylinder, the sixth empty so he couldn't accidentally shoot his own foot off while walking or riding. Now, he loaded a slug into both of the empty chambers. He might just be in need of two extra bullets.

Satisfied with his weapons, Sharper glanced quickly over to the livery stable to make sure Sandy didn't have any ideas on helping out and was safely out of sight. He saw no movement and hoped it stayed that way – whatever the outcome.

There was an alley to the right of the saloon that led off round back and into the desert. No point using that, he'd be a sitting target with nowhere to hide.

To the left of the saloon, the alleyway finished at a rough corral fence. The corral held three or four sad-looking ponies; beyond it was a small barn. That was better, he thought, if things got too bad he'd use that as a means of cover – or escape.

Studying as many of the seemingly empty

buildings as he could in the short space of time that was left before the riders hit town, Sharper saw no further movement: no twitching drapes, no doors being locked or bolted. Nothing.

There was a space behind the water trough and Sharper stashed his saddle-bags there, intending to retrieve them later.

Not that they contained anything of value, just his range stuff, spare matches, a clean, as yet unworn, shirt, some tobacco and a few odds and ends he couldn't even recall. But they *were* his.

Content that all was as well as it could be, Sharper removed his dust-laden rangecoat, displaying openly the two Colts, and sat on the edge of the boardwalk outside the locked saloon.

Reaching again into his vest pocket, he pulled out his tobacco pouch and proceeded to roll a quirly. Anyone looking, and Sharper was sure someone was, would think that there was a man with not a care in the world, having a smoke as the sun went down.

But inside, Sharper was tense, ready for whatever action might come his way.

He sealed the cigarette, struck a vesta with his thumb, and inhaled deeply.

The riders had slowed to a canter and, as he watched them approach, they reined in to a walk as they hit the far end of town.

There were six of them. One had a rifle drawn from his saddle scabbard and displayed it an angle across his chest.

These riders meant business, Sharper thought, and a sardonic grin spread across his dried lips as he took another draw on his cigarette.

A big man, who rode point, held his hand up, and the riders halted not more than a good stone's throw from where Sharper sat, Stetson pulled low, cigarette dangling from an almost invisible mouth.

The riders fanned their horses out a ways so that they had every angle covered, but Sharper sensed that the men felt no danger. They were so confident of their own superiority as shootists as to almost not pay Sharper much heed.

One of the riders cocked his Winchester and, from beneath the rim of his Stetson, Sharper saw that the rifle was aimed straight at him.

TWO

From her position in the livery stable, Sandy could see nothing. It was dark and dank, business not having been that good in a long while.

Mouldy straw covered the floor and, although she couldn't swear to it, Sandy was convinced the place was full of rats – or worse!

Having removed King's saddle and covered him with a blanket, Sandy had hooked a nosebag over his head full of oats: the horse was content.

Leaving her hide-out, Sandy crawled forward to try and get a look-see at what was happening outside.

O'Cready's rifle, an old Henry, was propped inside one of the stalls. Sandy grabbed it, not even checking to see if it was loaded. She felt more comfortable having a weapon.

The clapboards to the front of the livery were old and warped – just like the rest of the town – and there was plenty of room between the slats to get more than a good view.

Slowly raising her head, Sandy took a quick

peek; Sharper was still sitting on the boardwalk opposite, and, to her left, she could see the riders.

Two she recognized; Ben Robson, and his foreman, Luke Packard; the other four were strangers, but she knew them to be the Henry gang.

And what strangers: she had never in all her life seen such disgusting riders as the ones she now stared at. Even at this distance – thirty or forty feet – their filth was apparent. She could almost smell their grease-encased clothing, the beards each of the four wore were long and unkempt, hiding most of their faces. Three were jet black, the fourth, bright red.

The four men seemed to be dressed identically; the typical long rangecoat covering most of their bodies, drawn back to reveal sidearms, with the exception of one rider who held a Winchester rifle. Their horses didn't look in much better condition.

The sun, now sinking fast behind the six riders, painted each and every one of them a black silhouette: they looked like riders from hell, thought Sandy.

*

Sharper took a final draw on his cigarette and threw the butt into the street without even giving the six men a further glance.

Ben Robson eyed the relaxed man in front of him carefully.

That he was a stranger, Ben was in no doubt; but what was he doing here? Had Casey hired him to do his own dirty work? Or was it happenstance? All Ben Robson knew was revenge. Revenge for the death of his son, and his own personal hell of losing the only woman he'd ever loved.

'You're new 'round here, mister.' It was a statement, Sharper noticed, not a question requiring an answer, so he gave none.

'You deaf, boy?' Robson went on.

'Nope,' Sharper replied calmly even though that word *boy* grated something awful.

'I said you're—'

'I heard what you said, didn't see no point in answering the obvious,' Sharper said.

Ben Robson glared at the seated figure, the fury inside him already fit to boil over.

'You got any sense, mister, you'll mount up an' find yourself another town to drift into.'

'Kinda like right where I am.'

'You want me to kill him there, Mr Robson?' The voice came from Jack Henry, the youngest of Jud Henry's sons, he with the drawn and aimed rifle.

'You could try it, *boy*!' Sharper responded, still sitting on the boardwalk.

'Best you move on, mister.' This time it was Luke Packard who shoved in his two cents' worth, eager to please and hoping that, with young Sam out of the way, the Big B would one day be his; he had a lot at stake.

Ben Robson ignored Luke and, instead, spoke to Jack: 'Put your gun up, I'll tell you when and where.'

Jack grunted dismissively, but he kept the rifle aimed at the seated man – just in case he was given the slightest opportunity to plug him.

'This ain't no concern o' yours, mister,' Ben Robson went on, 'you take no mind to interfere, 'less o' course, old Malone sent you in?'

'I don't know no Malone,' Sharper said softly.

'Then we'll be about our business,' Robson said flatly.

'An' what business would that be?' Sharper asked.

'Seems I have to say everything twice to you, mister, it ain't *your* business, so you keep your peace.' Ben Robson was getting a mite agitated at the careless and relaxed manner of the stranger.

For the first time, he began to study him carefully; tall, rangy, with a dark stubbled face and the most piercing stare he'd ever seen. The man showed no fear, he showed no concern at being outnumbered six to one and, Ben saw, he wore *two* handguns.

This man sure wasn't no cowpoke, Ben thought. Maybe he *was* a 'slinger?

Luke saw his boss's hand move to his sidearm and thought it about time he showed his loyalty; loyalty he gave – for a price.

Without warning, Luke went for his pistol. Although fast, he wasn't that fast, and Sharper, already expecting something, was balancing on a hair-trigger.

Without moving his body a single inch, he drew and fired in one, quick, smooth action.

The force of the .45 slug lifted Luke clear from his saddle, throwing him backwards and his sidearm screamed uselessly into air before dropping to the ground. Unfortunately for Luke, if the bullet hadn't already killed him, the shock to his mount sure would.

Luke's left boot got stuck in its stirrup and the animal bolted, wide-eyed, ears pinned back, straight down the street in the direction from which they'd just ridden.

The animal was strong and Luke's surely dead body bounced like a rag doll from side to side amidst a cloud of ever-rising dust.

The five remaining riders hadn't moved a hair. Their own mounts snorted some, but, under the guidance of the men, they weren't allowed to bolt.

Sharper's smoking pistol was still held firmly in front of him, pointed now at Ben Robson.

'I didn't want no trouble, mister,' Sharper said, 'but if you can't control your men—' He shrugged, leaving the sentence unfinished.

'Well, you sure bought yourself a whole bunch of it, mister,' Ben Robson said through gritted teeth. 'We'll be back!'

'Name's Sharper, Sharper Wade, and I ain't goin' nowheres.'

With that, Ben Robson wheeled his mount and

set out at a gallop. Sharper wondered whether he was going after the body of his foreman, or not, but the remaining four riders stood their ground for a few moments.

'Like the man said,' Jud Henry repeated, 'We'll be back!'

'Look forward to that, mister.'

'Henry's the name, Jud Henry. You jus' remember that. These here are my boys. And, we will be back.'

Sharper grinned. 'Small town.'

The four men slowly wheeled their mounts and, at a walk at first, followed Ben Robson. As they reached the edge of town, they kicked into a canter.

Sandy emerged from the livery stable and stood in front of Sharper, her gaze following the riders.

'They don't seem to be in too much of a hurry,' she said.

'Nope,' Sharper replied.

'You think they'll come back?'

'Sure as the sun sets at night and rises again in the mornin',' Sharper said.

'Are you stickin' around?'

'Reckon so.'

'Ain't you a-scared none?'

'Too tired and hungry for that,' Sharper said and for the first time grinned at Sandy.

She blushed slightly as she saw his cold features melt and caught the flash of his teeth in the dying light.

'Best you get fixed with board and lodging,' she said self-consciously, her hands fidgeting. 'Sure think the café will open up again soon.'

'Think you're right there, little lady.' Sharper moved to retrieve his saddle-bags, then turned to Sandy: 'You make sure my horse was fed?'

'Uh-huh,' Sandy nodded. 'Gave him a bag o' oats.'

'Oats! That'll spoil him, he'll expect them from now on!'

Sandy wasn't sure if he was joshing her or not. 'I'll give him oats as long as you stay here,' she said, trying to be helpful.

'You do that an' he won't ever eat grass again,' Sharper said but – Sandy noticed – he was still grinning.

Sharper turned and headed across the street to the boarding-house without turning back to Sandy.

She was all but giggling to herself, like a school-child – and Sharper knew it!

*

Ben Robson grabbed the reins of Luke Packard's horse and brought the animal to a halt.

It didn't complain too much, and ducked its head down to nibble on the almost non-existent coarse prairie grass.

Robson dismounted and, with his stomach churning at the thought of the sight that he knew would greet him, he grabbed Packard's boot and wrestled it free of the stirrup.

The freed leg hit the dirt limply, a sickening squelchy sound, and Ben Robson took a deep breath before turning to the rest of Packard.

The black Stetson was missing, and Cogan's face rested in the dirt, for which small mercy Robson was grateful. His waistcoat was up over his shoulders and his shirt – what was left of it – covered the back of Packard's head.

The flesh revealed, Cogan's left side and most of his back was stripped of skin; muscle and sinew showed clearly and Robson, hard man that he was, almost gagged.

He'd skinned many an animal, that was part and parcel of living in the West, but to see a man skinned was something Robson could do without.

Still, he had to make sure the man was dead. Kneeling beside the body, Robson peeled back a flap of the shirt and the sight that greeted him would haunt him for months.

Packard's face had disappeared. Where, on his back, only the skin was missing, the face that now grinned up at him had had not only the flesh ripped away, but the muscle, too.

The skull showed clearly, glistening sickly white-red in the last of the sun's rays. One eye socket was completely empty the other had the eyeball hanging loose. The lips were gone too, and a set of teeth clamped round a pink tongue were exposed. While Robson had only gagged earlier, this time, bile built up in the pit of his stomach and he turned his back on the body and threw up.

There was no need to check for life signs. His foreman was dead.

Recovering just as the Henrys reined in, Ben Robson unrolled his blanket, grabbed his lariat, and proceeded to wrap Luke Packard's body.

'Shit!' Jefferson Henry said, 'you see that? Dang near took all his head off!'

'Yeah, OK,' Robson muttered.

'Ain't never seen nothin' like that,' Jack said and dismounted for a better look.

'Hot dog! He ain't nothin' but bone up there,' Jack said. 'Come see.'

'This ain't the time or place,' Robson spat. 'Show some respect, boy!'

Jack jumped to his feet, his pistol drawn.

'Don't you *ever* call me no boy, mister. I don't care who you is, I'll blow your head off, for sure.'

'Put the gun away.' The flat tones of his father, Jud, cut through the air. 'Now!'

'Aw, Pa!'

'I said, now!'

'Shoot.' Jack reluctantly reholstered his weapon.

'Now give Mr Robson here a hand with wrapping up that body afore ev'ry buzzard for miles around starts a-swoopin' in.'

'Why's it always me that gits the dirty stuff, you never git John or Jefferson—'

'Do as I say, boy.' Jud cut him dead with a black stare that even made Ben Robson shiver.

Jack fell silently to tying the lariat round the blanket and, between them, they tied what was left of Luke Packard to his horse.

'Come on, let's ride,' Ben Robson said as authoritatively as his queasy stomach would allow. He was sure the gang had noticed he'd thrown up, but he hoped not. Losing face to these low-lives was not a thing he wanted. Not at all.

*

Sharper was shown into a room that contained a single cot, a chest of drawers that had seen better days, atop which stood a bowl and pitcher.

There was a blackened mirror opposite the bed, a threadbare rug on the floor and hook behind the door.

'Dollar a night. Food's extry, so's laundry. No visitors, an' I lock the front door when the saloon closes. Dollar a night,' she repeated. 'In advance.'

Sharper reached into his saddle-bags and retrieved a small string-pull pouch. He opened it and handed over a dollar.

'You got no washin'?'

'No ma'am, reckon I'll git that down to the barber's when I get me a hot tub an' shave.'

'The hell you will.' Maisie Brown was in her fifties, fat as an ox and twice as mean, but with a heart of gold – when she wanted. She'd eyed Sharper from behind closed drapes, just like the rest of town, and wished she was thirty years younger. But she wasn't going to let *him* know that. So she gave him hell.

'Seems I can make up my own mind on that, ma'am.' Sharper said civilly.

'Ain't been no barber here past few months. Ain't here now, an' won't be here tomorrer. What you say to that, fella?'

'Seems I ain't gettin' no shave or hot tub,' Sharper conceded.

'Didn't say that, did I?' Maisie stared up into Sharper's deep eyes.

'Well, jus' what is it you *are* sayin', ma'am?'

'First off, I ain't your ma'am nor anyone else's. Name's Maisie, Maisie Brown, take it or leave it. Second off, I got me a tub, an' I kin shave you closer than an' Injun scalping Custer. It's—'

'Yeah, I know, it's *extry*,' Sharper said taking off the woman's voice.

'You got it, mister.'

'Name's Sharper Wade.'

'So what I call ya, Sharper or Wade?'

'Depends; you Maisie or Brown?'

'Like your spunk, Sharper.'

'Like yours, too, Maisie.'

'Tub'll be an hour. Food first. Ya hungry?'

Sharper nodded.

'Then git them boots off, wash up an' we'll eat.'

'Yes ma'am.'

Maisie glared at him, her sparkling blue eyes alight with a fire she hadn't had in many a long month.

'I ain't no ma'am!'

'No, Maisie, you ain't.'

She turned and grinned the biggest grin she'd grinned for years.

'Grub's coming up, young Sharper.' And she closed the door behind her.

Sharper stripped off his vest and shirt and poured water into the bowl. A bar of lisle was nearby and he commenced to scrubbing at his face, then shoulders and arms, feeling the strong soap invigorate his skin.

Looking round, he could see no towel.

Then the door opened, and a smiling Maisie stood there as if she had planned it – which she had – holding a clean towel.

'Thought you might need this,' she said.

'Bet ya did, Maisie. Bet ya did.'

She smiled at him, taking in his muscular torso, a clean fine physique, she thought and, as Sharper dried himself, old Maisie licked her lips.

'Stew'll be ready soon,' she managed to say and closed the door once more.

Sharper grinned to himself. The older they get, the worse they get, he thought, and then dug out the fresh shirt from his saddle-bags, slicked back his hair and left the room to see if Maisie could cook as well as she could talk.

*

Sandy Cogan stood in her room staring into the

full-length mirror that her uncle, Casey Malone, had given her for her eighteenth birthday.

Gone were the denims and boy's shirt: instead, she wore a gingham dress with bright white buttons that ran down the front and a pair of pumps she only ever wore if there was a barn dance – which was not that often.

She piled her hair high, saloon-girl fashion, and was applying the last of her rouge to lips and cheeks. The scent of lavender filled her room and she felt like a woman again.

She just hoped the man she dressed for noticed that too.

THREE

Ben Robson brought the body of Luke Packard back to the Big B.

With the drive under way, there were very few hands around the ranch; to be precise, only three.

Ben Robson had started ranching nearly thirty years ago, having moved out West with the early settlers. Sam, his only son, had been conceived during the arduous journey

As Ben dismounted, dropping the reins to Luke Packard's horse, thoughts of those past thirty years flashed through his head: the good times and the bad. A smile creased his wizened face as he gazed at the old barn; he remembered the day they'd finished building it, he remembered the night he'd spent there with his w—

Tears welled in his old grey eyes. His wife dead, now his son, and to top it all, one of his oldest friends

Ben couldn't see the sense of it all: what now, was the point.

Hate.

That was what he was now filled with. Hate. Hate of the country that had killed his wife, hate for Malone who'd killed his son; and now hate for the stranger who'd killed his friend and foreman.

The Henry gang sat atop their mounts staring first at the old man, then turning to each other; a silent message seemed to pass between them.

Jud Henry gazed around the spread: the ranch house, an imposing building, totally out of character with the rest of the buildings, the three barns, corral, and paddock were impressive.

An old-timer was repairing one of the fence rails, and Jud assumed there would be some sort of housekeeper around, but, apart from that, the place seemed deserted. He grinned.

Jud dismounted and his three sons followed suit. 'You figure on buryin' him here?' Jud said to Ben.

'Yeah.'

'Boys'll give you a hand, if'n you like.'

'No. I'll do it. He was my friend. I'll bury him.'

'Suit yourself, mister. Guess me'n the boys'll git some grub.'

Ben seemed not to hear, his head still swimming in thoughts of his life.

'That OK?' Jud called out.

'What? Oh, yeah, help yourself to food an' whatever. Kitchen's back o' the house.'

'You got a cook or what?' Jud asked.

'Nope. You'll have to fend fer yourselves.'

Jud glanced at his sons: they got the message,

loud and clear. Maybe, Jud was beginning to think, it was time to settle down, plant some roots again. Ease up on his saddle-sores.

'Come on, boys,' he said, 'you heard the man. Jack, sort out some grub.'

'Goldarn it, Pa! Why me?'

' 'Cos you're youngest and cookin' ain't fer menfolk,' Jefferson said, laughing.

The four men left their animals tied to a hitching post that stood in front of the four steps which led to a veranda running round the front of the ranch house.

Ben Robson watched as the four walked straight in through the front door. Contempt filled his face; the men hadn't even seen to their horses first.

He was beginning to have second thoughts about the four. Sure, they had a fearsome reputation: robbers, murders, rustlers, some even said rapists and Indian killers, but he felt, now that he'd met them, that they were far more dangerous than he had need for.

Dragging his thoughts back to the job in hand, Ben entered the barn, grabbed a pick and shovel, and led Luke Packard's horse down to the south field.

*

Maisie *could* cook as well as she could talk. The beef stew and dumplings, gravy soaked up with fresh-baked bread was the best meal Sharper had had for weeks – months, even.

The conversation had been light, Maisie hadn't asked too many questions, but she sure was checking him out.

'Where're ya headin'?' she asked nonchalantly.

'Nowheres in particular,' Sharper replied mopping the last of the rich beef gravy.

'Stayin' round long?'

'Maybe. Maybe not. Depends.'

'On what?'

'You're askin' a lot of questions all of a sudden,' Sharper said by way of reply.

'Hell,' Maisie said, 'only polite conversation. If I didn't ask nothin', you wouldn't say nothin'.'

There was a silence. 'So, depends on what?'

'May have escaped your notice,' Sharper said calmly, 'but I killed a man out there.'

'Sure I noticed,' Maisie said, waiting for Sharper to continue.

'I'd like to find out what's goin' on 'round here, what made him draw on me.' Sharper wiped his mouth with the back of his hand and moved as if to stand.

'You want coffee? It's fresh brewed,' Maisie said, hoping to prolong his stay at the table.

'Sounds fine, ma'am – Maisie,' Sharper corrected.

'I'll get the pot.' Maisie stood, cleared away the dishes and scooted into the back kitchen, lest he changed his mind.

Sharper relaxed at the table; belly full, he was now in dire need of a shave and hot tub, but he guessed those would come all in good time. He looked around the front parlour. The solid oak table wasn't from these parts, he thought, and the matching dresser was a fancy piece of carpentry, the open shelves at the top filled with plates and bowls, cups and saucers, and a few ornaments.

The rug on the floor was thick and obviously new. Sharper smiled as the realization hit him that old Maisie didn't usually treat her guests to this particular room.

The walls were covered with hand-painted paper and there were a couple of paintings; one of a gent with a thick moustache and sideburns, the other, a country scene from somewhere, but nowhere round here, Sharper thought.

Maisie entered the room, coffee-pot in one hand, fresh milk and sugar in the other. She set the items on the table, crossed to the dresser and pulled down two cups *and* saucers.

'Mind if I smoke, Maisie?' he asked.

Maisie hesitated for a second: the last and only person to ever sit and smoke in this room had been her long-dead husband. She glanced at the portrait on the wall, and then at a big armchair that nestled in the corner.

Sharper turned to look at the chair: on one armrest sat a newspaper and a pipe, to one side were a pair of slippers.

'Sure,' she said finally. 'Why not.'

Sharper thanked her and rolled himself a smoke; as he lit up Maisie placed an ornate ashtray in front of him, then proceeded to pour the coffee.

'Milk? Sugar?'

'No, thank you, Maisie, just as it comes.'

They sat in silence for a while, Sharper sipped at the hot brew and began to feel he ought to say something.

'That your man,' he said, indicating the painting.

'Sure was. Ol' fool died eight years ago. Still miss him.' She sighed and sipped at her coffee.

'The sheriff,' Sharper went on. 'He on the level?'

'Casey Malone?' Maisie laughed. 'That ol' fool. Straight as a die. Nothin' ever happens in this town. Only excitement we ever get is a wagon-train or a drive, an' they ain't that often these days.'

'You know what happened over to the saloon?'

'Sure. Everyone knows what happened. Sam Robson got too big fer his britches and forgot hisself. Drew on Casey. Sheriff had no choice: it was shoot or be shot. He shot.'

'Never been any trouble between the town and the Robsons?'

'Only the usual, you know, wantin' to be the big boss an' all. Ol' Ben's not a bad person, but losin' his wife an' son, well, that's enough to change any man.'

'Guess it is,' Sharper agreed.

There was silence again.

'What about Sandy?' he asked eventually.

Maisie grinned. 'What about her?'

'Well, she said Casey was her uncle. Where's she livin' now?'

'Back o' the jailhouse, same as ever.'

'That don't seem a fittin' place to live,' Sharper said.

'Why, ain't no jail there.'

Sharper grinned.

'Anyhow, she'll be over directly.'

'Sandy?'

'Yup.'

'She often here?'

'Every night since Casey went.'

She studied Sharper's face, watching for a reaction. The only one she got was a slight lifting of one side of his top lip, but that was enough.

'More coffee?'

Sharper nodded and she poured.

The door swung open and Sandy bounced in.

Sharper couldn't believe his eyes. This was no tomboy, he thought. This was a real, honest-to-goodness *woman*!

*

Jud Henry sat at the large pine table that stood in the middle of the Robson kitchen. He leaned back, put his boots on the table and pulled out a cigar stump he'd been saving all day.

'Seems we got some rich pickin's here, boys,' Jud said puffing out a stream of acrid smoke.

John, second eldest and first dumbest, stared open-mouthed at his father. 'How come, Pa?'

Jud Henry ignored the boy; if it wasn't for the fact that he was the quickest of any of them on the draw, Jud would have dumped him years ago.

'Jefferson, Jack, reckon we could settle here, real comfortable like.'

'Sure could, Pa. How ya wanna do it?'

'Reckon the ol' man'll be an hour or so yet, we'll let him finish up an' eat with us, then we'll finish *him* up!' Jud chuckled.

*

Ben Robson knew his land, he knew exactly where Luke would rest in peace.

The south pasture had a fine view and the sun shone for the most part of the day. Luke would rest well here, the old man thought.

Halting the animals, Ben dismounted, grabbed the pick and shovel, and commenced digging a grave for his old friend.

After thirty minutes of hard slog, Ben reckoned the hole was deep enough. He rested up, got his breath back, and dragged a bandanna across his forehead and the back of his neck. He stretched long and hard, the ache in his back was another symptom of his age he thought, as he reached for the body of his friend.

The rest didn't take him long. Filling in the hole was sure a whole lot easier than digging it out.

He fashioned a cross and thrust it into the ground; then as he turned to go, he thought he'd better say a few words.

Not being a religious man, he wasn't familiar with anything he could quote from the Good Book, so his words were unspoken, but from the heart.

As he stared at the mound and the cross, his anger resurfaced. He had to avenge the death of his friend; and there was no time like the present.

Leaving his digging implements – he'd collect them later, he patted the rump of Luke's horse, the stallion would find his way home and Barney, his old handyman, would see to him.

Ben mounted: eyes steely, jaw-line firm, he'd made up his mind. He'd hunt down the stranger that'd killed Luke and gun him down like the animal he was!

*

The sound of approaching hoof-beats roused Jud Henry from his reverie. He walked to the front of the house and peered out from behind the drapes.

'That him, Pa?' Jefferson asked.

'Seems like a riderless horse,' Jud answered. 'Now where in hell is ol' man Robson?' Jud rubbed his stubbled chin with a hand that hadn't seen water in a long time.

'Want I should ride on out and check him?

Might have had an accident, or something,' John offered.

'For once in your life you come up with a good idea, John. Take a looksee, fast.'

John left the ranch house and Jud watched as he rode out. 'Dang fool don't even know where the old man went,' he mutted under his breath.

But John wasn't *that* stupid. He'd seen the direction from which the horse had come and the tracks were still fresh.

It took him no more than ten minutes to find the grave. He dismounted, grabbed the pick and shovel and, for reasons known only to him, stashed them across the back of his saddle.

Bending, he sussed out Robson's tracks.

Soon, he was back at the ranch house.

'Looks like he done rode into town, Pa,' he said.

Jud looked at the boy; contempt, pity and sorrow flickered across the big man's face for a split second before, 'How d'you know that, son?'

'Obvious, Pa. Tracks led that way.'

Jud grunted: he'd asked a damn fool question.

'What'll we do now, Pa?' John asked.

'What we do now, boy, is we eat.'

*

Ben Robson rode at a steady canter. He wanted to gallop, to get to town as fast as he could before, maybe, his courage failed him.

He was mad – real mad – a red haze hung

around his peripheral vision. All he could think of was shooting and killing the stranger.

He couldn't understand, and in this state of mind, didn't pay much heed to this feeling he had. He seemed to feel angrier about the killing of Luke than he did for his son. Or maybe, he thought, the frustration at not being able to find Casey Malone and the fact that the stranger was still in town – his brain halted.

Supposing the man had ridden on out?

Ben Robson formulated a plan. If the man had gone, he'd use the Henry gang as planned. Maybe get the sheriff and then go after the stranger. Yeah, he thought, that'd do.

The town loomed up on him before he even wondered where the gunman might be. The saloon was closed. Al Green, the owner, deciding he really needed to visit his brother after the shooting of Sam Robson.

He reined up his mount and an evil grin lit his lips, his eyes stayed icy-cold.

Maisie Brown.

Had to be, he thought, Maisie Brown's boarding-house. Nowhere else he could be.

Robson dismounted, tied his horse to a rail and checked his weapon. Six slugs. More than enough, he thought as he reholstered.

He pulled his Stetson down firmly on his head and he walked across the deserted street, glancing to his left and right as he went.

He came to halt outside the boarding-house

and exageratedly flexed the fingers of his right hand. Realizing he still wore his riding gloves, he hurriedly removed them and flexed his fingers again.

Should he just barge on in? Call out, he decided. But what if the man wasn't there? He'd soon find out, he thought.

Maybe he should loose off a shot first, attract some attention, and then call him out.

Ben Robson had never shot a man in his life and, only for his anger, he wouldn't be here now, doing what he was about to do.

Even so, the tendrils of fear he felt crawling up his spine weren't enough to stop him now. This was for Luke – and Sam – he added mentally.

Taking out his pistol, he shot twice into the air, then reloaded.

In the silence of the town, the shots echoed, and seemed to reverberate back off every building. The silence afterwards was eerie.

For a few moments there was no movement; not from the boarding-house, the saloon or anywhere he could see. A few drapes twitched, and Ben caught the movement out of the corner of his eye. But he didn't turn; he stared at the front door of the boarding-house with a gaze so intent that everything else just disappeared.

Maisie was the first to react.

Glancing at Sharper, she moved across to the side of the window facing the street. Peering round the edge of the closed drapes, she saw Ben

Robson standing slap-bang in the middle of the street.

'Oh, Lord!' she said, half to herself.

'What is it?' Sharper asked.

'Seems like Ben's after callin' you out, mister,' she said and turned to face him. 'He ain't no shootist.' Her eyes held a silent plea.

'You reckon he's after me?' Sharper asked.

Before Maisie could answer, a bellow came from outside: 'You comin' out, mister, or do I have to come on in and get ya?'

'Don't do it, mister,' Maisie said.

'He's callin',' Sharper said, and reached for his gun-belt.

FOUR

Ben Robson felt a pain in his chest, but chose to ignore it. His breathing was laboured and sweat broke out on his forehead and ran in streams down his face.

Too late to back off now, he thought, and dragged the back of his hand across his eyes.

His rage was beginning to wane, he knew that, but he had to go through with it.

Slowly, the front door of the boarding-house opened and the tall, slim figure of Sharper was silhouetted in the doorway.

Ben Robson swallowed.

'You after somethin', mister?' Sharper's voice betrayed no emotion.

'I'm callin' you out, stranger. You killed my foreman.'

'I shot in self-defence, mister. I got no quarrel with you.'

'Well I sure as hell have a quarrel with you!' Ben Robson's voice shot up an octave.

'Mister, whatever has bin goin' on here, ain't none o' my business.' Sharper's voice was firm, and Ben could see the twin Colts back-lit from the boarding-house.

'I'm makin' it your business now!' Ben's voice had a timbre of control to it.

'I ain't drawin' on you, mister, an' that's flat.'

Sharper stood, feet slightly apart, both hands gripping the buckle of his gun-belt. He knew he was back-lit, but he didn't want to move into the darkness for fear of making Robson do something he'd regret.

'Ben, you get back to your ranch now, y'hear?' Maisie stood behind and slightly to one side of Sharper.

'You git back inside, Maisie Brown, I don't wanna have to shoot you as well,' Ben said.

'Do as he says, Maisie,' Sharper said without turning.

'You ready, mister? Or you a yeller-bellied no-good skunk?'

Sharper had to grin. He knew his face was in darkness and that Robson wouldn't see it. But that was the oldest trick in the book.

'Mister, I ain't a-risin' to your name-calling.'

'Then you best git ready,' Robson said. 'I'm a-countin' to three.'

And with that, Ben Robson began his count.

'One—'

'Back off, mister,' Sharper said.

'Two—'

'This is your final warning!'

'Three—'

Ben Robson grabbed for his gun. The sweat that had been running down his face was also running down his arms. The palms of both hands were sticky and wet.

Maisie was right, Sharper had time to recall, he sure wasn't no shootist.

But, shootist or not, if he drew and fired, Sharper knew he could still get himself killed.

Robson's draw seemed to go in slow-motion. It gave Sharper plenty of time.

Robson's gun was out now, held none too steadily in his right hand. He swept his left hand across to cock the chamber and, in one swift, easy movement, Sharper drew and fired.

Both men's guns went off at the same time.

Then silence.

The silence was broken by a shriek from behind Sharper.

Robson heard the scream and, for a few seconds, still on his feet, wondered what the hell was going on.

Sharper replaced his weapon; Robson's seemed to fall slowly from his hand. The fingers wouldn't obey his brain.

Ben Robson watched as slowly, the gun fell to the ground.

Ben Robson followed it.

It seemed that all hell had broken out inside the boarding-house. Sharper turned after watching the old man fall, and went back inside the house.

'What's goin' on? he asked.

Maisie was kneeling by the body of Sandy Cogan. She didn't say anything, just looked up at Sharper with tears in her eyes.

'Sandy? How?'

'Slug passed straight through the wall, I guess' Maisie said and pointed to a small hole behind Sharper.

'She bad?'

'I don't know, I ain't no sawbones,' Maisie said.

Sharper gently moved the woman to one side as he knelt by Sandy's body.

At first, he could see no sign of any wound. Then the tell-tale stain of red began to seep through.

'There a doc in town?' Sharper asked.

'On my way,' Maisie said and left the room.

Sandy was breathing; a good sign, Sharper thought needlessly. The stain was seeping through her dress low down on the left side. Taking out his Bowie knife, Sharper, as gently as he could, began cutting through the material.

Relief swept over him as he exposed the wound. The bullet had passed straight through, nicking the flesh for an inch or two. Sandy must have fainted, Sharper thought.

Using the cut material, Sharper stanched the now gentle flow of blood and waited.

For the first time in the less than four hours

that Sharper had been in town, he heard voices
out on the street and the sound of running footsteps.

Maisie came crashing into the room followed by
a rickety-looking old man who looked as if he
hardly had the strength to tote the black leather
bag he carried.

'This here's Doc Holliday,' Maisie said, and
added as Sharper opened his mouth, 'No, it ain't
that Doc Holliday.'

The old man knelt by Sandy Cogan and opened
up his bag.

'Just a flesh wound, Doc,' Sharper said. 'I'll go
check on Robson.'

'Oh, Lord,' Maisie said, 'I clean forgot about
him!'

Outside, Ben Robson lay motionless, eyes wide
open, he was staring up the stars.

'You OK?' Sharper asked.

'You shot me in the leg,' Robson said.

'I know.'

'You could've killed me,' Robson said, his voice a
monotone.

'I know,' Sharper repeated, 'but I didn't aim to
do that.'

Ben Robson closed his eyes and almost smiled.

Sharper quickly inspected the wound. It wasn't
serious, but the old man would be off his feet for a
while.

Doc Holliday joined Sharper outside and
patched up Robson's leg.

'You're lucky, Ben,' he said. 'Ain't serious.'

'Luck had nothin' to do with it,' Ben replied. Doc Holliday didn't bother to ask why.

A small knot of the remaining townsfolk had gathered. Doc Holliday got some of them to carry Ben over to his surgery, and said: 'Someone fetch my buggy, so I can take Sandy over as well.'

'Sandy? What's wrong with Sandy,' Ben asked.

'You shot her, that's what's wrong with her,' Doc Holliday answered.

'Oh, God,' Ben moaned. 'She hurt bad?'

'Naw, just a nick. She'll be fine. Good job it was you doin' the shootin',' the doc added.

*

Jack and Jefferson found the whiskey – not that it was difficult to locate. A whole crate of it was stashed in the pantry.

Jud smacked his lips as he helped finish the first bottle. Stomach full, a whole box of cigars to choose from and enough whiskey to drown a mule.

He was in pig heaven.

'John, take a ride into town, quiet like, an' see what's goin' on, and pass me another bottle.'

'What'm I lookin' fer,' John asked petulantly.

'See what ol' man Robson's up to,' Jud said; the whiskey had mellowed him some.

'An' do what?'

'Then come on back an' tell me about it,' Jud replied, his voice showing impatience – he hadn't had *that* much whiskey!

'Yeah, well, jus' you all make sure there's some o' that whiskey left fer when I git back.' John stomped out of the ranch house and mounted up.

Jud continued to drink, along with Jack and Jefferson.

It didn't take John long to reach town. Although the animal hadn't been fed or watered yet, it was a good, strong horse – it had to be.

He reined in at the edge of town. Oil-lamps flickered in the gloom and he could see three or four people standing outside the saloon. As far as he was aware, everyone had skedaddled when Robson had made his threat. So how come some folks were still in town? he wondered.

He tied his horse outside the livery, opposite the saloon, and the grateful animal lapped at the water still in the trough.

John sat on his haunches and watched the three men outside the saloon. He could hear their voices, but not what they were saying.

He decided to get himself a drink.

He stood up, crossed the street, ignoring the now silent trio, and climbed up on to the board-walk to enter the saloon.

'No good tryin' that,' one of the men said. 'Saloon's closed.'

'When's it gonna open?'

'Hell if I know,' the man replied.

'Well, we'll see about that,' John said and took out his pistol.

'Al's away,' another man said. 'He won't take too kindly none to having his place all shot up.'

John turned to face the last speaker. 'You figure on stoppin' me, mister?'

'Hell no,' the man said and the trio began to edge away.

'What about you two?'

'Ain't our saloon, mister,' they answered.

John grinned, knowing the three were scared of him. 'Then get your sad asses outa here,' he said, cocking his pistol.

'Ain't no need—'

John aimed his Colt and fired. The speaker flew backwards, landing with a thump in the middle of the street.

He was dead before he hit dirt.

The other two men, overcome with shock, went for their guns, but they were too slow. Far too slow.

A maniacal grin on his face, John fired twice more.

Three men lay dead in the street.

Sharper heard the shots and then silence. He was standing by Sandy as Doc Holliday finished cleaning and bandaging her wound.

'What the—' Holliday began.

'Stay put, Doc,' Sharper said. 'I'll go check it out.'

A fourth shot rang through the air and Sharper drew both his pistols.

'Be careful.' It was the first words Sandy had uttered. Both Sharper and Doc Holliday looked towards the girl they both thought was in a dead faint.

'You feelin' all right?' Sharper asked.

'A bit sore. What's going on?'

'That's what I aim to find out,' Sharper said. 'Now you rest up, I'll be back.'

Replacing one of his guns, Sharper leant across and kissed Sandy gently on the cheek. 'You hear? Rest up.' With that, he left before Sandy could say more.

Outside it was pitch black and Sharper stood for a while to get his night vision.

A few minutes later a lamp was lit in the saloon and, as the weak yellow light filtered out through the now open doors, Sharper saw three bodies lying in the street.

FIVE

The sickly yellow light that spread more gloom than cheer on to Main Street, only vaguely illuminated the three still bodies.

Sharper drew both handguns, cocking them automatically. The metallic click as the well-oiled mechanism slid into place was strangely reassuring.

Eyes now used to the darkness, Sharper moved to the nearest body and, kneeling, felt for a pulse in the neck with his little finger. Not once did he look at the man; his eyes were fixed on the smashed front door of the saloon and the still swinging batwings.

With his own pulses racing, Sharper made sure the man was dead before moving to the next man. Again, the result was death.

The third man, however, was visibly breathing. A dry, rattling sound was coming from the man's throat and even in the darkness, Sharper could see a thin trickle of blood running from the corner of the man's mouth, down his chin, before disappearing beneath his shirt.

'You hear me?' Sharper whispered.

'Uh-hu,' the man managed.

'I'll get you some help. Any idea who' was doin' the shootin'?'

The man coughed, and a bubble of blood crept from his mouth.

'It's OK,' Sharper said, 'reckon I'm about to find out.'

Standing to a crouch, still keeping his eyes fixed on the saloon, Sharper waved to a couple of people who were watching from a safe distance.

Neither man made as if to move.

Backing up slowly, Sharper neared the townsfolk.

'That man is still alive,' he gritted. 'Now git over there an' take him to the doc's!'

The two men looked at each other and Sharper could hear them both swallow deeply.

'Now!' he added, and the two men rushed across the dirt to roughly drag away the wounded man.

'Be careful,' Sharper said, 'you kill him an' I'll be lookin' for ya!'

The two men slowed down now; both seeming to think that if the gunman in the saloon didn't shoot them, this stranger sure would!

The street was empty now. Sharper knew his every move was being watched from the safety of houses and stores and he figured the only sort of help he was going to get in this good-for-nothing town, was resting in both palms and made of metal.

It was obvious that whoever had done the shooting was pretty sure of himself. As Sharper neared the saloon entrance he could see the man clearly, leaning up against the bar drinking.

Sharper released the hammers simultaneously and reholstered. He'd play this one by ear.

Crossing the street, arms hanging deceptively loosely by his sides, he stepped up on to the board-walk.

Inside the saloon, the man paused, shot glass in mid-air as he heard the sound of the creaking boardwalk.

Slowly, he lowered the glass on to the bar top and almost imperceptibly his right arm slipped down his side, hand resting on the butt of his six-shooter.

Sharper paused outside the batwings and stared into the saloon; John Henry could feel eyes piercing the back of his head.

Deliberately, he turned to face the saloon entrance, elbows resting on the bar top.

Sharper recognized the man.

'You comin' in fer a drink, or me?' John said casually, as if either reason suited him.

'Depends,' Sharper said. He used his body to open the batwings as he moved inside, thereby keeping his arms by his side.

'Well, if it's a drink yer after,' John Henry said, 'looks to me as if it's on the house tonight.' Then he stood straight. 'If it's me, I'm here, stranger.'

'Guess you shot those three men yonder,' Sharper said.

'Guess I did.'

'You got a reason?'

'Never had one afore, don't see no reason to have one now.'

'Then it's you I've come for,' Sharper said.

John Henry, using his left hand, picked up the shot glass and emptied its contents down his throat in one go. He threw the glass over his shoulder, dragged his hand across his lips and hooked both thumbs in his gun-belt.

'Don't see as how it's any o' your business, mister.'

'I'm making it my business.'

'Then make your play,' John Henry said. At the same time he drew.

Sharper had expected the move. He was only surprised the man hadn't drawn while he drained his glass.

The slug creased Sharper's left arm, high up, as he, too, drew and fired simultaneously.

Even in the relative darkness of the saloon, Sharper could see the look of both shock and surprise, as two slugs caught John Henry in the chest, thudding him back against the bartop.

The man kept upright, whether through his own strength or the bar counter, Sharper didn't know, but he didn't fall – at least not straight away.

The look of surprise was still on John Henry's

face as he looked at his own sixgun, as if it were faulty.

He was still looking as the gun fell to the floor, grazing the spittoon, before clattering to the floor-boards.

John Henry's head sank to his chest as Sharper watched, and he seemed to slither, rather than fall, to the floor.

Sharper Wade replaced the Colt in its left holster, as the graze in his arm began to sting, but he hadn't lived this long to take any chances by holstering both weapons.

He walked forward and kicked the discarded weapon further away from the slumped form of John Henry, before lightly kicking the man.

The body – for that's all it was now – fell side-ways: it was the last move John Henry would ever make.

*

Outside, the street began to fill with the few folks still around.

Sharper could hear the murmuring of people who weren't quite sure what was happening, or who had survived, and none of them was in an all-fire hurry to find out.

Making sure the dead gunman was just that – dead – Sharper replaced his gun and gripped his left arm. The sting began to make its presence felt now, and Sharper saw no reason not to help himself to a shot of whiskey while he composed himself.

He'd faced many men in his life; some by his choosing, like now, others where situations had just developed, and every time, Sharper reckoned, could be *his* last.

Using his right hand only, he filled a tumbler and sank the cloudy amber liquid, feeling it burn its way down his throat. The second shot was more leisurely as the pain in his arm became a dull ache that he could ignore.

Behind him, he heard the squeak of the batwings opening and, by intuition, he knew he didn't have to turn.

'You OK, mister?'

Sharper didn't recognize the voice, but he answered anyway.

'Yeah, I'm OK. How 'bout the other feller outside? He make it?'

'I'll go take a looksee,' the man said and disappeared.

Footsteps, followed by a cough, approached Sharper and a heavy, black leather bag was plonked on to the bar top.

Doc Holliday didn't say anything as he proceeded to help himself to a whiskey.

'Good to see ya, Doc,' Sharper said.

'You hit?'

'Just a crease, don't 'mount to much,' Sharper replied.

'Will do if'n blood poisonin' develops from the

lead,' Holliday said, and poured another shot for both of them. 'Take your shirt off, else I'll cut it off.'

Sharper drained his glass and didn't argue.

The townsfolk were feeling braver now. Seems like the right man had won the gunfight after all. One by one they shuffled into the saloon giving Sharper friendly looks, but most of them were intent on the whiskey.

Holliday ignored the mêlée of the now brave dozen men whose voices got louder in proportion to the amount of whiskey they drank. He patched up Sharper's arm and commenced to repack his bag.

'It ain't over, son,' Holliday said.

'Reckon I know that, Doc,' Sharper said. 'How's Sandy doin'?'

'She's OK, just needs time and rest.'

'And Ben Robson?'

'That ol' coot? He's as quiet as a church mouse. He'll be fine, if'n I keep 'im on his back a few weeks.'

Holliday took another shot of whiskey. 'You stayin'?'

'Hell no, don't want the barkeep to bill me for his missing whiskey.'

Both men left the saloon unnoticed by the now raucous townsmen.

Outside once more, the heat of the day had slowly disappeared and Sharper thankfully sucked in a lungful of the cooling air. He had managed to survive again, and he was thankful for that.

*

Jud Henry was far too drunk to wonder what had delayed Ben Robson – or indeed why John hadn't returned.

Seemed Old Robson kept himself plenty of liquor and Jud was content; with his belly full and the stove stacked up he mellowed in his new-found comfort and wealth. For he was sure this *was* going to be *his* comfort and wealth.

His two sons were asleep in the kitchen, mouths wide open, snoring fit to wake the dead. He looked at both of them and the thoughts that ran through his head weren't fitting for a father to consider about his kin.

He sighed and reached for the bottle. Damn kids, he thought, can't take their liquor. Not like me.

He brought the bottle to his lips and took a slug. His head sagged and the bottle slipped from his fingers as he, too, fell into a drunken slumber.

*

The sun rose at four of the a.m., and a shaft of light shot through a gap in the drapes directly on to Sharper's eyes. Instantly, he was both awake and alert.

The dull throbbing in his arm had kept him awake for a while, but sleep had overcome him. Now, it was no more than a slight inconvenience.

Maisie had not bothered him when he'd returned the night before. She knew what had happened and what he'd done. But the two dead men were innocent townsfolk who only toted a gun to shoot off rattlers and the occasional cougar, driven by hunger from the mountains.

Maisie was not stupid.

What her guest had done was more than any man in the town would have done, and for that, she was grateful.

She just wished she was twenty years younger.

The smell of fresh bread and bacon sizzling was all the excuse Sharper needed to get out of bed.

'Mornin',' Maisie said as he entered the kitchen.

'An' mornin' to you, Maisie,' Sharper said. 'That sure smells good.'

'Glad to hear it, it's ready.'

The meal was consumed in silence, even though Maisie had a million and one questions already lined up and waiting to leave her mouth like a flash-flood.

Sharper finished eating and picked up his coffee-cup.

'Maisie, that was pure heaven.'

'Glad you liked it.' She looked bashful and even blushed slightly. 'Your arm all right,' she asked, hoping that maybe the bandaging was loose or needed replacing. Even though she was old enough to be his mother – big sister, she corrected herself – it sure would be nice to see a male body again, even if she could only look.

Sharper grinned a thanks and said it was fine, nothing to worry about.

Maisie, although disappointed, smiled back, but her smile vanished.

'You know it ain't over, 'less'n you ride on out.'

Sharper drained his coffee-cup and Maisie refilled it.

'You an' the doc must be in league,' Sharper said, 'he tole me tha same thing.'

'Well, that's two of us with some sense,' Maisie said, and started clearing the dishes away.

Sharper reached in his vest pocket, pulled out his tobacco-pouch and set to rolling a quirly.

'What keeps you here,' Maisie asked, 'as if I didn't know already.'

'If'n you know already, why ask?'

'Jus' makin' sure, is all,' Maisie said.

'Makin' sure o' what?'

'You want more coffee?'

'Sure.'

Maisie poured out the coffee and Sharper lit his cigarette, inhaling deeply.

'I'll visit Sandy and Ben,' he said after a pause.

'You plannin' on stayin' around?'

'Can't see no reason to leave. Can you?'

'I can think o' three,' Maisie said. 'You know as well as I do that once Jud Henry gits to hear you done killed one of his sons, he ain't gonna come ridin' on in here to thank you. Goddammit!'

'No, maybe he ain't. On the other hand, I can't see as riding' on is gonna save this township a whole mess a trouble. Can you?'

'Maybe not,' Maisie agreed, 'maybe not.'

SIX

'How're you feelin'?' Sharper asked as he sat on the edge of the bed gazing at Sandy.

'Better now you're here,' she replied.

Sharper grinned.

'Doc told me what happened,' she added.

'Yeah, well, I couldn't just ignore it now, could I?'

'No, I guess you couldn't.'

Sandy went quiet, before, 'I also guess you'll be movin' on.'

'Nope.'

Sandy's face brightened, then she frowned. 'But you know the Henry gang'll be lookin' for you.'

'Reckon they will. But I ain't runnin',' Sharper said, his eyes steely.

'This isn't your fight, you know.'

'Seems everbody's keen on tellin' me that,' Sharper said and helped himself to a coffee.

'Then why stay?'

'Nowhere better to go to just yet, so I'll stick

around awhiles. You seen Ben yet?' Sharper said to change the subject.

'No, he's in Doc's front parlour, but I sure hear him a lot.'

'How's that?'

'He's been a-hollerin' all day. Wants to get back to his ranch. Doc says no way can he be moved yet, but Ben's worried. The Henry gang's holed up there.'

'Maybe I should take a ride out there, check it out for him.'

'I don't think that'd be a good idea,' Sandy said and went to grab hold of Sharper's hand, then changed her mind.

Although she knew very little about this man, she had a soft spot for him that was growing bigger by the minute.

He was a saddle-tramp, for sure. Never settled in one place for too long, and Sandy, young as she was, didn't want to scare him off just yet.

Sharper drained his coffee-cup and stood up.

'I'll just check in on Ben, see how he's doin'. You take care, now.' He smiled down at Sandy, and for a moment, she thought he was about to kiss her. Instead, he ruffled her hair.

'I ain't no school kid!' she said indignantly.

'No, ma'am, you sure ain't,' Sharper said, still smiling as he left the room.

'About time you showed your face,' Ben Robson said irritably. 'Sit down and fill me in, son. What's been goin' on? Doc's tole me a little, you tell me the rest. I may be wounded and not much use to you, but that don't mean I can't do something to help out.'

'Good to see you too, Ben,' Sharper said as he sat in a big armchair that was opposite the sofa Ben occupied. 'Glad to see you ain't too ill.'

'Sorry, son. I'm jus' all-fired up, is all. There's only old Barney out at the ranch, an' I know I made a big mistake in hirin' them Henry boys.'

'What's done is done,' Sharper said.

'I gotta get back, but the doc, he says no.'

'If the doc says no, then no it is. You want me to take a ride out there?'

'I can't ask you to do my dirty work,' Ben said.

'You ain't askin', I'm offerin',' Sharper replied.

'You got fixed up with a job yet?' Ben asked.

'I ain't had time hardly to take a shave in this town, never mind anything else.'

'Will you work for me?'

'Let's see how things pan out, first. OK? Anyone in town I can rely on?'

'You jus' gotta be kiddin' me,' Ben replied. 'Sheriff's run off, along with 'most everyone else. I know, it's my fault. But Sam was my only boy, an' what with my wife—'

'So it's me or no one,' Sharper said. He'd already figured on that, but he needed the confirmation.

*

Jud Henry was the first to wake up; mainly

because he fell off the chair he'd collapsed in the previous night.

His yells soon brought his two sons back to the land of the living.

'Shit! My head's a-hurtin', Pa,' Jack said and buried it in his hands.

'Where's John?' Jud Henry pulled himself up from the kitchen floor and, bleary-eyed, looked about the room.

'I said, where's John?'

'How the hell are we s'posed to know. You sent him off, didn't ya?' Jack said.

'He shoulda been back by now,' Jud said.

'Yeah, well, 'less'n he got hisself laid, or he's upstairs, he ain't back,' Jefferson said, backing up his brother.

'Go check upstairs, an' if he ain't there, check out the stables.'

'Jesus!' Jefferson stood up, he knew it was pointless arguing with his old man.

'An' you,' Jud yelled at Jack, 'fix me up some coffee an' grub.'

Jack just groaned, but he, too, knew arguing was useless.

He threw some more wood on to the stove and disappeared into the pantry.

'He ain't upstairs an' his pony ain't in the stable,' Jefferson said as he plonked back down in his chair by the table.

'Then go find him,' Jud said.

'Let me have a coffee an' some grub first, then

I'll go,' Jefferson said. 'If he's in town, he'll be back, an' if he's dead out there on the trail, another thirty minutes ain't gonna make no difference any whichway.'

Jud didn't answer straight away, his head was now pounding like a herd of buffalo and what Jefferson said made sense.

'OK, we'll eat, then we'll take a ride into town.'

*

Sharper returned to the boarding-house to be greeted by Doc Holliday and Maisie.

'Seems like I'm gonna have some more guests,' Maisie said.

'Sandy and Ben?' Sharper asked.

'Ain't got the room down at my place,' Doc Holliday answered. 'Got that Jim Hollins there now, ain't got me a place to hang my hat.'

'Jim Hollins?' Sharper looked puzzled.

'That was the feller that survived the shootin' last night,' the doc added by way of explanation.

'Doc reckons you stay around much longer, we'll have to build ourselves a hotel,' Maisie added and burst into a long and loud laugh.

'I'll give you a hand, Doc,' Sharper said.

'Got my buggy ready,' Doc said.

'Let's do it! Maisie, we'll see you later.'

Doc and Sharper left Maisie to get the two rooms ready. Doc drove and Sharper rode shotgun.

They rode in silence for a while. The surgery-cum-veterinary house was at the far end of town. A small, neat building, complete with white picket fence and a small plot where Holliday grew some herbs and vegetables.

'What you plannin' on doin', son,' Holliday said eventually.

'Seein' things go all right,' Sharper said.

'For who?'

'For me, Sandy, you, ole Ben Robson. You need anyone else? When Jud Henry finds out I killed one of his sons, he won't rest till he takes me out. If I ain't around, this town's a heap o' dust an' everyone in it's dead.'

*

Casey Malone had been riding for a day when regret bit deep into his soul.

He'd run scared, leaving Sandy alone.

It was time to make amends. He'd shot in self-defence and he owed Ben Robson both an apology and an explanation.

Casey made up his mind. He *was* the sheriff, goddammit!

After sleeping under the stars for the first time in God knew how long, Casey lit a camp-fire to warm up. He'd left town in that much of a panic that he had no coffee, no food, nothing.

Stretching his aching limbs, he readied himself for the day's ride back to Robson's ranch.

He lit himself a cigarette and sat by the fire, soaking up the little warmth it offered, and prepared to face his own personal hell.

*

It took Doc and Sharper only five minutes to load Sandy on to the buggy and take her back to Maisie's boarding-house.

It took considerably longer to move Ben Robson.

'I tell you, Doc, I'll be as right as rain back at my own place,' he said.

'You ain't goin' back yet,' the doc said. 'I don't know how many times I have to say it: you cain't go back till your leg gets a damn sight better. Understood? Maisie will take good care of you and we'll sort out the ranch.'

Ben Robson clamped his mouth shut and offered as little help as he could in getting over to the boarding-house.

Once they were both settled, Sharper left them to their own devices for a while. Maisie was in her element anyway, fussing and clucking like the mother hen she was.

Sharper had to be alone for a while and plan his next course of action.

The saloon doors were still open and, as he pushed his way through the batwing doors, he saw the place was deserted.

Good, he thought, some peace and quiet.

It was still too early in the day for whiskey, so Sharper helped himself to a beer and sat at a card table in the far corner of the saloon, a table that couldn't be seen by anyone glancing in through the open door.

Placing his beer on the table, he reached into his vest pocket and pulled out his tobacco-pouch. Not much left, he though but enough for a cigarette now; later he'd visit the general store and fill up.

Relaxing for the first time that day, Sharper pondered on what might happen. The Henry gang would come to look for John, that much was certain. But when? Should he confront them? Or wait and see?

He knew he couldn't rely on getting any help from the townsmen, and the sheriff had disappeared. Maybe it would be better to wait for the Henry gang to ride in.

Decision made, Sharper drank his beer and smoked his cigarette.

Thoughts of Sandy drifted in and out of his mind as he smoked. He was confused by the feelings he had for the girl – young woman – he corrected himself and a small smile crept on to his lips, which he quickly doused.

Beer and cigarette finished, Sharper decided to check on King. With Sandy out of action at the livery, and O'Cready still away, he decided to water and feed his mount and give him a good grooming.

It would be a while before there was any action

made by the Henrys, he thought, so he could take his time. Another thought hit him: he didn't even know the name of this town.

*

Unseen by Sharper, his every movement was being closely watched.

Django Whitman was a failed man. He'd run a café and corral in the good old days when the wagon trains were frequent.

Cattle used to run through Main Street at a rate you couldn't count, and Django was one of the richest men in town.

Then, his wife left him, the café burned down and the cattle drovers found quicker and easier routes to get their animals to market.

Django lost everything. But now he had a plan; a plan that would get him rich again, and all he needed was a little help.

The Henry gang was the little help he needed.

SEVEN

The thirty minutes that Jud and his sons had delayed leaving for town had now turned into over four hours – and they still hadn't left.

The noonday sun burned fiercely in a clear blue sky. The sands danced and shimmered as the heat rose. There was no wind, and the heat was relentless, thirst-making – whiskey-drinking weather. And there was plenty of whiskey to be drunk.

Jud's whiskey-addled brain decided for him that they'd best wait for the cool of the evening before setting out for town. Jefferson moaned some, but not for long. Jack just followed his father's lead.

Taking a wander round the ranch house, Jud was even more convinced that this was where they would settle.

Even to his uncouth eye, the presence of a woman's influence was there. The drapes, rugs and furniture showed that.

Taking a swig straight from the bottle he addressed his sons: 'This, boys,' he said, 'is more like it.'

'More like what, Pa?' Jack asked.

'You dumb critter!' Jud replied. 'I'm fixin' t' take up residence, boy. It's time we planted some roots.'

'We're gonna farm?' Jack said, shock on his face.

Jud swigged from the bottle again, and disdained to reply, but his eyes looked up to the ceiling. Just once, he thought, I'd like me a conversation with someone who had half a brain. He drank again.

The knock on the front door brought him back to the present.

Drawing his gun, he motioned for Jefferson to open the door.

Outside, Barney stood, hat in hand, waiting for his breakfast.

'Yeah?' Jefferson spat.

'Mr Robson here?' Barney asked.

'Nope.'

'He comin' back?'

'Hell, I don't know.'

'He does my breakfast,' Barney said, 'usually brings it to the bunk house, but it ain't there an' I been a-waiting.'

'Well, he ain't here,' Jefferson said and slammed the door shut.

Barney stood on the front porch for a short while, wondering what to do. He was hungry. Maybe he ought to rig up the buggy and go to town. Maisie'd look after him.

He replaced his battered and torn hat and turned to leave. The only thought on his feeble mind was getting fed.

Inside, Jud felt like side-swiping his eldest son.

'You dang fool, what you let him go for?'

'He's jus' an old man,' Jefferson replied.

'He may be an old-timer, but now he knows something's up.'

Without waiting, Jud threw the front door open and fired – twice.

Barney felt a sting in his shoulder, then his feet left the ground as the second slug tore his spine apart.

He landed hard; what breath was in his old lungs exploded from his mouth and Barney found he couldn't suck any more in.

He couldn't move. His eyes could see, his face could feel the heat from the sun's rays hitting it, but he couldn't move a muscle. Then there was a salty taste in his mouth and as he looked at the dirt that was only an inch away from his nose, he saw the red stuff pooling, sinking in and drying at the same time.

His body twitched uncontrollably, and the bright, white light, darkened into black, but Barney hadn't closed his eyes.

*

Casey had ridden hard. He'd pushed his horse

before he changed his mind and drifted off into the wilderness. He was the sheriff and he wanted – no, needed – to remain being the sheriff. It was all he had left.

He reined in to give the animal a rest. Flecks of foam covered its flanks and Casey felt sorry for it.

Stopping, he took his canteen from the saddle-pommel, dismounted, removed his hat and emptied the contents into it. It wasn't much, but the horse was grateful; his big brown eyes looked straight at Casey as his large pink tongue lapped up the warm water.

Using his bandanna, Casey wiped the foam from the neck and flanks and the horse whinnied in appreciation.

'Sorry, boy,' he said out loud, 'I bin all-round stupid.'

The horse nudged him as if to say it was OK, and Casey grinned.

Remounting, he rode the animal at a steady canter; it would be another two hours before he faced up to Ben Robson. He could do without water for that long.

*

At the same time, Sharper had finished grooming King. Fed, watered and fussed over, the animal was content.

As he turned to leave he was confronted by Sandy.

'What in hell are you doin' out here?' Sharper asked.

'I had to come and see you,' Sandy said, avoiding his steely gaze.

'I'm takin' you straight back to Maisie's an' no arguin'.'

Sandy didn't argue. She was more tired than she'd thought and, with Maisie fussing in the kitchen, Sandy had thought it too good an opportunity to miss. But now she had Sharper's attention, she was glad to be led back to bed.

'So, what was so all-fired important you had to come see me?' Sharper asked as he led her out of the livery stable.

'I – I just needed to see you, that's all,' Sandy replied.

Sharper had his arm around her shoulders helping her to walk and, she was was quite sure, she felt an almost imperceptible squeeze of his arm.

'I was goin' to call in later. I'm stayin' at Maisie's too, you know.'

'I know. I just didn't want you riding out to Ben's ranch and – and maybe not comin' back.'

'I ain't ridin' anywheres 'til the Henry gang makes a move. I ain't a lawman, but, so far as I can make out, they ain't broke no laws yet – 'ceptin John, o' course, an' that's bin settled.'

'You *know* they'll come a-lookin',' Sandy said.

'Wouldn't you if the boot was on the other foot?' Sharper asked.

Sandy nodded.

'Don't you worry none,' Sharper said, placatingly. 'Things have a habit of turning out OK. You'll see.'

*

Django Whitman watched as Sharper led Sandy Cogan back to Maisie's rooming-house. His mind made up, he knew what he was going to do.

He mounted up, and set off to meet up with the Henry gang and put his plan into operation.

The ride took less than an hour, but the heat of the day was tiring and Django reined in about a quarter of a mile from the ranch house.

He wiped the sweat from his face and pulled a slug from the nearly empty whiskey bottle he carried in his saddle-bags.

Courage was beginning to fail him. What if the Henrys laughed and just shot him? Why should they? He had important information for them.

He threw the now empty bottle to the ground and scanned the ranch. Nothing moved, but as he gazed into the horizon, his eyes lifted to the cloudless sky.

Funny, he thought, don't usually get buzzards circling so close in. He half dismissed it as maybe a dead steer that had attracted them. Then he remembered the drive had already started. Maybe a horse then, he thought.

Maybe not, his senses told him, but he rode on. Walking his horse on, he gradually neared the ranch house, and that's when he saw the body that had attracted the buzzards.

It was close to the ranch house, that's what had kept the birds a-circling, he thought.

From inside the house, Jefferson watched the rider approach, stop, and stare down at the dead man.

'Got ourselves another visitor, Pa,' he said in a whisper.

'Ain't no need to whisper,' Jud slurred back at his son. 'No one can hear yer.'

Rising from the comfortable chair Jud had claimed as his own, he crossed the room to the window.

'Now who in hell's that? Go take care o' him, Jefferson.'

Jefferson grabbed his rifle, slid his hat on, and walked towards the front door.

'Hello, inside!'

Jefferson halted in his tracks, waiting for his father to tell him what to do.

Jud sighed. 'Seems like he wants to parley.'

Jud grabbed his own rifle and, ignoring both Jefferson and Jack, stormed to the front door.

Flinging it open wide, Jud stepped on to the veranda; his two sons stood slightly back and to either side of him.

'Mr Henry?' Django called out.

'Who wants to know?'

'Name's Whitman, Django Whitman, an' I got some bad news, Mr Henry.'

Jud Henry's eyes closed to slits as he eyed the rider. 'An' what bad news would that be?' he asked eventually.

Django Whitman kept both hands in full view, showing he wasn't trying to start any gun-play. He swallowed deeply, the sweat breaking out afresh, although it wasn't just the heat that brought it on.

'Seems he got into a fight,' Django said.

'Who?'

'One o' your boys,' Django simpered.

'And?'

'Seems he got hisself killed over to the saloon.' Django waited for an explosion that never came.

His grip on the reins was turning his knuckles white. He knew that, even if he managed to wheel his horse about, the chances of him getting away unscathed from three men with rifles was pretty damned remote.

'You see who done it,' Jud asked, his voice calm, but filled with a deep menace.

'Stranger by the name of Sharper Wade.'

'You best come explain, boy,' Jud said, and Django visibly relaxed as he saw the rifles being lowered.

Kicking in his heels he walked his animal forward, tied up at the hitch rail and dismounted.

Jud's eyes never left the man as he approached.

Django removed his Stetson and mopped his brow again. 'Sure is hot, Mr Henry.'

'Sure is,' Jud said. 'Now explain.'

When he'd finished telling Jud and his two sons about the shootings, Jud stood silently for a while, then: 'What about Ben Robson? You seen him?'

'Sure, he's over to the rooming-house, along with that Cogan girl Wade's sweet on.

'Seems ol' man Robson came lookin' for Wade an' Wade shot him. He was good though, shot him in the leg.

'I kinda got an idea, Mr Henry, if you an' your boys are interested.'

'Always interested in ideas, mister,' Jud said. 'You best git inside, now.'

Django's nerves were twitching like a bust termites' nest as he climbed the steps to the veranda. What sort of a man was this that didn't grieve the death of one of his own sons?

Inside the kitchen, the four men sat round the big wooden table. Jud was silent, waiting for Django to start.

'Mind if'n I help myself?' Django motioned to one of the whiskey bottles.

It was Jefferson who slid the bottle across the table.

'Thanks.' Django took half a dozen gulps before putting the bottle back on the table.

'Figured you might wanna get even with this Wade feller,' Django said at last.

'Dang right we—' Jack started, but Jud raised an arm to silence him.

'What's on your mind, mister,' Jud said in a toneless voice.

'Well, I kin help you out there,' Django said.

'In return for what?' Jud demanded.

Django picked up the bottle again, but quickly replaced it as Jud drew his hand-gun.

'I'm waitin',' was all Jud said.

'Well, like I said, I can help you there. I know the town, I know where this Wade feller hangs out an', well, way I see it, you get maybe to kill him an' maybe one or two other folks—'

'What other folks,' Jud said, his curiosity rising as to the man's motives.

'Well, way I see it, maybe we could do a deal, on the town, like. You know, carve it up between us. Let me run the saloon, an' maybe be mayor.'

Jud grinned. 'What's to stop me a-doin' that anyways?'

'Well, as I said, I kin look after our town for us, an' with ol' Ben Robson out of the way—'

'We git the ranch as well, huh?' Jud said.

'But ain't that what—?' Jefferson began.

'Shut your mouth, boy,' Jud said.

'An' I figure,' Django went on, his confidence building now, 'that if we was to maybe take the girl, bring her out here, that would make Wade come on out after her.

'He won't get no one to ride with him. But if we was to ride in after him, well, some of the folks there might jus' feel like protectin' their property. There's only four of us.'

'You say the girl and ol' man Robson's in the same place?' Jud asked.

'Sure is,' Django replied.

Jud sat silently, then leant forward and picked up a whiskey bottle and drank deeply.

'An you wanna be mayor and have the saloon?'

'That's all,' Django said smiling.

'Mister, we ride at nightfall. We'll take the girl and take care of Robson.'

Django grinned, almost splitting his face in half. He picked up the other whiskey bottle and, holding it towards Jud's, clinked the glass.

'Here's lookin' at you, mister.'

'Lookin' at you back, mister,' Jud grinned, but Django couldn't help noticing the man's eyes weren't grinning.

EIGHT

Jud Henry sat and drank, all the while his black eyes never left the face of Django Whitman. He was a patient man – with three, no two – stupid sons, he'd had to be.

Django's unease had gradually drifted to the back of his feeble brain as the whiskey took a hold of what few senses he had left.

He was laughing and joking in a voice that was too loud, too forced, in an attempt to befriend the three killers he faced round the kitchen table.

Both Jack and Jefferson went along with Django, Jud noticed. Damn fools, he thought. Bad enough having to carve up the place with his two remaining sons without splitting any more with Django Whitman.

Sunset fell and exposed a blue-grey full moon that wiped out the blood-red rays and coated the prairie with a grey light and blacker than black shadows.

Jud sat and watched and waited and all the

time he was formulating a plan: he didn't know what yet, but he had the vaguest idea struggling to come out.

John was dead.

Jud sighed, took another slug of whiskey and sighed again. Ah, well, he thought. It had to happen sooner or later. Maybe he had to go get that stranger in town? What the hell was his name? No matter, he decided, dead men don't need no name. He grinned to himself, unseen by the other three.

'Better break out some steak,' Jud said to John. 'We got us some ridin' to do come sundown.'

*

Sharper escorted Sandy back to the boarding-house in silence now, Sandy forgetting her sore side as Sharper's arm rested across her shoulders. She gazed into the dusky sky as the sun began to dip behind the distant mountains and the full moon took ascendancy.

Already, small pinpricks of twinkling light began to fill the darkening sky as stars made their presence felt.

Romance. That's what was running through Sandy's mind at that moment.

Danger. That's what was running through Sharper's mind at that moment.

If he were in the Henry gang, night would be the time he made a move. Darkness was an ally as well as an enemy, he thought. He'd already decided on a plan of action. He was riding out to the Big B.

Maybe he could take them out there, save any bloodshed in town. If he succeeded all would be well, if not— Well he let that thought drift off. He wouldn't be around to find out.

They climbed the four steps to the veranda of the boarding-house and Sandy halted and half-turned to face him.

She lifted her head and gazed into Sharper's eyes.

He looked down into hers and saw the woman she was. For a fleeting second, all danger was forgotten.

'Thank you for seeing me back safely,' Sandy almost whispered.

Sharper cleared his throat and swallowed. He'd had plenty of women in his life: some good, some not, some remembered, some forgotten, but all left behind. But there was something about this woman that made him feel uncomfortable, awkward, and he didn't know how to handle it just yet.

'My pleasure, ma'am,' he managed.

'Are you coming inside yet?'

'Er, well, I guess I'll take a walk round town first,' Sharper replied. 'I need to make sure they ain't already here.'

It was a lie: he knew it and Sandy knew it, but she let it go.

'My side's kinda painful,' she said eventually. 'I guess I'd better go rest up awhiles. See you later?'

'Sure, I'll call in afore I go to bed.'

She knew that was a lie as well, she knew he wouldn't be sleeping that night.

Reaching up, she gave him a small kiss on his cheek. She lingered a while and Sharper knew it was an invitation to respond, and he almost did.

'You two staying out there all night?' Maisie boomed as the front door of the boarding-house was flung inwards; a yellow glow from the oil-lamp she was holding spilt out across the veranda.

Sharper straightened and Sandy took an involuntary step backwards.

There was a wicked gleam in Maisie's eyes as she stared at the obviously embarrassed couple.

'You, young lady, should be a-restin' up. I made some beef tea so's you better come get it afore it gets cold.'

'Yes, ma'am,' Sandy replied, her eyes fixed firmly to the wooden boarding beneath her feet. She swept past Maisie into the hallway.

'You plannin' on taking root there, Sharper, or are you comin' in?'

Sharper grinned and Maisie could see, in the dull light from the oil-lamp, that he was a touch flushed.

'I'm gonna take a walk round town first, ma'am – Maisie, then I'll look in later.' Sharper began to think straight once more. 'You make sure you lock

up. If – when I return, I'll knock three times on
the kitchen door, OK?'

'Don't you worry none about that,' Maisie said,
'This place'll be locked tight as a—'

Maisie was interrupted by a call from inside.
Ben Robson was obviously wondering what was
going on.

'Hold on to your breeches,' Maisie called over
her shoulder, 'I'm coming.'

She lowered her voice. 'You keep your eyes
peeled out there, Mr Sharper Wade, them Henrys
are a bad lot.'

Sharper tipped his Stetson. 'I sure will Maisie.'

He stepped off the veranda and waited while
Maisie locked, barred and bolted the front door.
He watched as the dim yellow light from the oil-
lamp disappeared, then he set off towards the
livery stable and King.

*

Casey Malone was only thirty minutes from town.
He'd walked his horse for the past hour, not wanting to tire the beast: he was without water and
feed and the little water he'd had in his canteen
he'd already given to his horse.

Doubts began to surface once more in Casey's
mind. Sandy was his main concern, but, he
reasoned, she'd be taken care of. Maisie would see
to that, he knew. But it was his job as sheriff that
the doubts centred around.

Sheriff for four years and, apart from a few drunks and a few petty robberies, he'd never had any real trouble in town.

Now, at the first sign, he'd ridden off like a deer with a cougar on its tail.

Casey swallowed dust and tried to lick his lips.

The sun sank and almost immediately a coolness hit the air. He stared at the moon, looking for inspiration, but none came.

He reined in and dismounted, stretching his legs, back and arms. It was a long time since he'd spent a day in the saddle, and it was beginning to tell on his old frame.

He wanted to do the right thing. But what if the right thing got him killed? Who would take care of Sandy then?

But if he'd continued to run, Sandy would be on her own anyway.

Casey was no hero, he knew that. He was no shootist, either, but was he a coward? His heart said no, but his brain disagreed.

Then he remembered the creek. Could only be about three, maybe four miles from here. He should water his animal. Yeah, he thought, water the horse an' me, an' then ride on into town and take whatever the good Lord had in store for him.

Decision made, Casey remounted, reeled left and set off at a walk: no sense in tiring myself or my horse, he reasoned. Maybe even sleep under the stars, ride in in the morning, come sun-up, horse refreshed, me refreshed. Be good and ready then. Good and ready.

With those thoughts in mind, Casey headed for the small creek that meandered out of the mountains before disappearing under the desert.

*

Django was asleep, his head resting on his arms, mouth wide open and snoring fit to wake the dead. Jud had managed to curb his intake of whiskey – which was more than could be said for his sons. He'd slept for a while on and off and was now getting himself mentally ready.

Jack had collapsed on to the kitchen floor, his unfinished steak sitting in its own fat on a now cold plate.

Jefferson had fared better. He'd at least made it into a bedroom next to the parlour.

Jud reached across the table and pulled Jack's plate towards him. He picked up the cold piece of meat, took a bite out of it, chewing slowly. Congealed fat and blood slid down his chin and dripped on to the front of his shirt, not that anyone would ever notice it. The shirt he wore, and had worn for longer than he could figure, was of indeterminate colour, except on the insides of his elbows; for some reason the red colour prevailed there against all the odds.

He threw the cold steak on to the floor where it landed next to Jack's inert body with a dull thud and slid into the boy's face.

He twitched his nose, coughed, licked his lips and one eye slowly opened. Then closed again.

'Coffee, boy,' Jud thundered.

Jack's eyes opened wide. He had no idea where he was. He struggled into a sitting position.

'Wha—'

'Coffee, now!'

Jack's left arm was dead from the shoulder down, his head thundered as a herd of stampeding buffalo ran behind his eyeballs and the demons in his stomach began jumping up and down.

The smell of the cold meat hit him at the same time as his arm began to come back to life, and then the demons found the buffaloes.

Jack threw up where he sat.

'Jesus Chris'amighty!' Jud yelled and aimed a tin mug at his son which missed and clattered across the kitchen floor. The door burst open and Jefferson appeared, gun in hand, trousers round his ankles, eyes staring wide.

'What? Wass goin' on?'

Jack stood, wiping vomit from his trousers and kicking out at the piece of meat at his feet.

'Nothin',' he said by way of reply, and opened the door to the wood stove. Light grey smoke filled the room as he poked at the dying embers before placing small pieces of wood inside. Inside five minutes, John placed larger logs into the stove, filled the coffee-pot and sat down at the table, resting his head in both hands.

Jud hadn't moved. Django was still dead to the world. Jefferson put his Colt back in the holster he was holding, placed them on the table and pulled up his trousers.

'Git ready, boys,' Jud said. 'Sun-up's due in a few hours, an' we're goin' to town.'

NINE

Sharper made a slight detour on his way to saddle up King. He needed to ensure that Doc Holliday knew what his plans were. Maybe, he thought, he should have informed Ben Robson too, so at least he would be on his guard, but that would have meant Maisie and Sandy knowing, and he knew they would have objected – strongly.

No, the best bet was Doc Holliday, he could visit Ben on the pretext of giving him a check-over and, between them, they could be on guard while he was out at the Big B ranch.

'Sharper, what brings you out?' Doc opened the door wide to allow Sharper to enter.

'Can't stop, Doc, I'm on my way out to Robson's place. Said I'd check out the Henrys for Ben.'

'That's a damn fool thing t—'

'Doc, I know what you're thinkin', but to my mind, attack is the best form of defence. You know they ain't gonna let up on Malone and they sure ain't gonna let up on me.' Sharper's steely eyes bore into the doc's.

'You goin' alone?'

'Can't reckon on no one else goin', can you?'

Doc Holliday coughed in embarrassment.

Sharper caught Holliday's embarrassment. 'Don't figure you Doc, that's not what I meant.'

'I know, it's just, if'n I was thirty years younger—'

'I know, Doc. Anyways, I figure it's better this way, maybe save bloodshed in town. I want you to let Ben know, without alarming Maisie and Sandy, maybe you could stay over.'

'Sure thing, Sharper. I'll get my bag.'

'Thanks, Doc, it'll ease my mind some.'

Sharper took his leave and continued on over to the livery stable.

*

Casey had got used to the dark now; in an hour or so, it would be sun-up and he fully intended to ride into town.

He'd ground-tethered his horse in a patch of lush grass fed by the creek, lit himself a fire and rolled a cigarette.

The sound of the running water and the gentle chewing of his horse had a soporific effect and, even though Casey didn't feel at ease sleeping out under the stars, his eyelids began to droop.

'A couple o' hours' sleep won't hurt none,' he said out loud. 'Maybe I'll build up the fire some and catch me a nap.'

Wood was aplenty by the side of the creek, washed down by the spring thaw, so it didn't take Casey long to gather the dry lumber and build himself a roaring fire – one that could be seen for miles around.

*

'Tie that critter up, Jack,' Jud said to his youngest son, 'and make sure you tie and gag him good.'

'Ain't he a-comin' with us, Pa?'

'No, he ain't a-comin' with us, I wouldn't trust that no-good bum any further than I could spit a rattlesnake in a dust storm. Now tie him up!'

Jack muttered under his breath and went to leave the kitchen.

'Where's that damn coffee?' Jud bellowed.

'You want coffee or you want him a-tied up? I cain't do the both things at once.'

'Git the rope, guess I can manage the coffee,' Jud replied.

'Big o' ya,' Jack mumbled.

'Say what?' Jud stood.

'I'm gettin' the rope, see, here's me goin' to get the rope.' Jack scurried outside.

Jefferson had finished pulling up his breeches and was fixing on his gun-belt.

'Git the coffee poured, boy,' Jud ordered.

'You jus' said you was gonna—'

'Never mind what I jus' said. Do it!'

Django farted, scratched his nose and snored even louder.

'Gag that sonofabitch!' Jud roared.

Django's eyes opened wide and he slipped off the chair, landing heavily on the floor.

'Wha—' was all he was able to say.

Jud rose from his chair and brought the butt of his pistol down across the side of Django's head.

The sound of both jaw-bone and cheek-bone cracking as Jud pistol-whipped him seemed to echo round the ranch house kitchen.

Jud leaned over the prostrate body of Django Whitman and tapped him none too gently with his boot.

'Well, that's saved a mess o' tying up, anyhow,' he said as he walked back to his chair. Jefferson filled two tin mugs with steaming coffee and joined his pa at the table, neither man being overly concerned about the welfare of the late Django Whitman.

Jack returned with the rope and commenced to tie up a dead man. He didn't even the notice the rapidly-spreading pool of blood around Django's head.

Jud just stared. 'Ya dang fool,' was all he could say.

*

Sharper saddled up and led King out of the stables. By his reckoning it was now way after midnight. The two and a half hour ride out to the Big B lay ahead of him, but he was unconcerned. To his way of thinking, the Henry gang would be sound asleep, he doubted that they'd even have anyone on look-out.

Mounting up, he took a glance down Main Street: blackness greeted him. Not a single light shone, save from the boarding-house.

Sharper gently dug his heels into King's flanks and set off at a walk.

Doc Holliday left his surgery-cum-veterinary-cum-house and stepped on to the boardwalk opposite Sharper.

'You take good care now,' the doc said in hushed tones.

'I will, Doc, you too.' Sharper tipped his hat and continued on.

The doc walked towards Maisie's without looking back.

'Who the hell's that?' Maisie roared from behind her front door.

Through the draped glass partition, Doc Holliday could see the outline of a Winchester pointed straight at him.

'It's me, Maisie, Doc Holliday.'

'You know what time it is?' her voice not losing any of its anger.

'I know what the time is, I promised Ben I'd look in,' Holliday said, unconvincingly.

The shadow behind the door moved and Holliday heard the bolts being drawn and the large iron key being inserted into the lock. The door swung open and a curlered Maisie, in a white cotton nightgown that covered everything apart from hands and head faced the doc with a scowl on her face that would sour milk.

'Who you think you're foolin'?' she said.

'I wasn't foolin' anyone,' Holliday croaked. Maisie intimidated him at the best of times, and this sure wasn't the best of times.

'Best come in,' Maisie said, and stood to one side. Doc Holliday entered and Maisie locked and bolted the door behind him.

'You wanna rest up that rifle a-ways?' Doc Holliday said, using a finger to move the barrel away from his chest.

'Not until you tell me what you're a-doin' here an' what's goin' on, I ain't!'

'There's ain't noth—'

Maisie moved the barrel up to Holliday's chin.

'Maisie!' Sandy, hearing the noise, had left her room and stood with a look of astonishment on her face.

'What on earth—'

'Something is happenin',' Maisie said. 'An' I intend to find out what.' She levered the Winchester.

'Now just a goldarn minute—' Holliday spluttered.

'Maisie, where's Sharper?' Sandy asked.

'That's what I'm aimin' to find out,' Maisie replied, not once taking her eyes from those of the docs.

'Well?' she said.

Doc Holliday swallowed hard. He *knew* Maisie wouldn't pull the trigger. He stared back at her. He swallowed again. At least, he *thought* she wouldn't pull the trigger.

'I'm waitin',' she said.

'He's gone out to the Big B,' he capitulated. Maybe she would have pulled the trigger.

Maisie lowered the rifle.

Doc Holliday breathed a sigh of relief.

Sandy moaned, 'Oh, no!'

And Ben Robson bellowed from his room: 'How's a body s'posed to get some sleep round here?'

Maisie opened the door to Ben's room and all three went inside.

'OK, Doc, spill it,' Maisie ordered.

*

'So that's how I figure it.' Jud finished explaining to his sons. 'So let's saddle up and git, we'll be in town afore sun-up.'

Jack and Jefferson both sighed, try as they might, they could never figure their pa's thinking.

Jud didn't give a hoot what they thought anyway; he saw a pot of gold waiting for him at the end of a rainbow. He could spend the rest of his life in the lap of luxury. Maybe, he thought, git me a woman, too.

'Horse's are ready, Pa,' Jefferson called from the front door.

'On my way, boy, on my way.' Jud pulled himself up from the comfortable chair, drank the dregs of his coffee, kicked Django once more to make sure, and he was sure; Django was stone dead.

'Dang fool,' Jud said and spat on the floor, watching as his spittle merged into the already congealing blood.

He left the kitchen, oil-lamps blazing, walked down the short hallway and through the front door. Pausing, he adjusted his gun-belt, breathed the cool night air deeply, and spat again.

'Let's have us some fun, boys,' he said and heaved himself atop his horse. Without waiting for his sons, he cruelly dug his spurs in and set off at a gallop.

Jack and Jefferson mounted, looked at one another without speaking, and set off in pursuit.

After twenty minutes, Jud reined his mount into a canter, his sons had caught up and followed suit.

'Pa,' Jefferson started. 'How come we don't jus' get rid of ol' man Robson?'

'I already tole you why,' Jud said impatiently. 'We need to get rid o' that stranger, too. He don't seem like no man who'll jus' go away. 'Sides, he done killed John. Don't that mean *anything* to you two idiots?'

'Sure it does, Pa,' Jack offered. 'But—'

'But nothin',' Jud hollered. 'We do as I say, you got that? I got this all figured. That, that fella, whatever his name is, will be beggin' for us to kill him.'

Jack and Jefferson exchanged glances again.

Jud reigned to sudden halt.

'What's up, Pa? Jefferson asked.

'Lookee,' Jud pointed ahead. 'Seems like a mighty big camp-fire.'

Jack and Jefferson peered through the gloom and saw sparks rising in the night air.

'Ain't no Injun', that's for sure,' Jack said.

'Well, let's take us a looksee,' Jud said, a grin flickering across his craggy face. 'Might make us a few cash dollars to boot,' he said as he sent his horse forward.

Jack and Jefferson followed on – as ever.

TEN

Sharper caught sight of sparks rising into the air.

He reined in and watched. He could see no movement, but it was still too dark and he was too far away.

He made a decision: he would not deviate from his mission; he would check out the Bar B and the Henry gang first, then, if he was still alive, maybe he'd take a look at whoever had lit the camp-fire.

Setting King into a light canter, he headed off to Ben Robson's spread.

*

Maise, Ben and Doc Holliday were in deep conversation, helped out no doubt, by the bottle of whiskey Maisie supplied.

Sandy silently edged out of the room; her disappearance wasn't noticed. She picked up Maisie's

Winchester rifle, silently left the boarding-house and made her way to the livery stable. Sharper would need help, she knew that, and if there was no man brave enough, then she would do it herself.

She saddled up her mare and walked the animal down Main Street, keeping to the shadows.

The rifle felt heavy and reassuring as she reached the edge of town, where she halted her horse and mounted up. She ignored the pain in her side as she slid into an unfamiliar saddle.

Once out of town, she set the horse to a steady gallop and made her way towards Ben's ranch, her resolve as strong as ever, but the dark night sky sent shivers down her spine.

In the distance, she too saw the sparks rising into the air.

*

Jud Henry was in no hurry. The food and the whiskey had slowed him down a touch and made him a tad mellow.

Behind him his two remaining sons followed at a canter, which began to irk: damn fool boys, he thought, ain't even got the balls to ride alongside me.

In the distance, the camp-fire still spewed sparks high into the night sky: Dang fool, Jud thought. Must be some kinda city dude to light a fire that big out in the wilderness. Serves him right if'n he gets hisself kilt. Jud grinned to himself.

'Get your asses up here!' he yelled suddenly.

Jack and Jefferson automatically dug their spurs in hard and caught up to their father.

'We split up here,' Jud said. 'No sense in ridin' in head on, critter might make a break fer it.

'Jack, you head south, Jefferson, break north. I'll ride straight in from here. You got that, OK?'

'Sure, Pa,' Jack replied. 'What we do then?'

'You wait 'til I give the signal.' Jud spat into the dirt, removed his bandanna and wiped a suddenly sweaty forehead.

'OK, Pa,' Jack said.

'An' what's the signal?' Jefferson asked.

Jud retied his bandanna, and breathed in deeply.

'Well, I guess you git to hearin' gunshots. That oughta to do it.'

'OK, Pa, you gonna kill him?'

'No. I'm gonna sit right down by the fire, there, and chew the fat!'

'Then why—'

'You jus' shut the hell up, boy!' Jud shouted. 'This is just a li'le ol' sideline here, boys. Put a few nickels and dimes in our pockets. Then we ride in to kill that there damn stranger fella, what kilt John. Now let's move!'

*

Sandy found the riding more difficult than she had thought. The constant jolting in the saddle - which was too big for her - was causing more pain in her side than she wanted to admit.

She gritted her teeth. Determination was strong, but she couldn't ignore the pain any longer.

She wheeled in her mount and rested awhile, leaning forward in the saddle to ease the throbbing in her side.

Clouds scudded high across the face of the moon, and what she thought was inky darkness turned even blacker.

Fear crept through her body. Fear of the night, and fear of what could happen to Sharper.

She rose up in the saddle as her eye caught the sight of a glow in the distance. She blinked. Making sure she wasn't just seeing things. But no, there was a glow; as her eyes got used to the dark she could see the sparks rising into the air before disappearing.

Casey?

Why had that name sprung into her mind?

Could be anyone, she told herself. Sharper? No, definitely not Sharper. It was away to the east, the Bar B was to the west, there was no way Sharper would have ridden that far off track.

The fire seemed too big for a camp-fire. Maybe it was the beginning of a range-fire. Not uncommon at this time of the year.

Should she ignore it and ride on?

The pain in her side throbbed as she rode, and that she did choose to ignore – at least for the time being.

If it *was* Casey, surely he could help. Indecision caused Sandy to rein in. The Robson spread was at least an hour away, and Sharper had had at least half an hour start on her. If she was to be of any use at all, she thought, she'd better get a move on.

Taking a deep breath, Sandy spurred her horse forward, If it was Casey, she would enlist his help; if not, then she would only have wasted ten or fifteen minutes.

She set off towards the camp-fire.

*

King cantered at a steady pace. The trail was good, flat and even, so despite the darkness, the big horse never faltered in his long, easy pace.

Sharper kept his steely gaze straight ahead. He was already surprised that the Henry gang hadn't ridden into town.

The mere fact that Ben Robson had disappeared he could overlook; but that one of the

Henry gang was also missing struck him as a tad peculiar.

No accounting for folk, he thought.

*

Jud reined in and tried to make out if Jack and Jefferson were in position. With his head still throbbing, Jud had used the camp-fire as a guide, and subsequently his night vision had all but disappeared.

As he peered into the inky gloom, all he could see was the image of the flames.

'Dammit to hell!' he breathed as he wiped his forehead with a bandanna that might once have been red.

Turning back to the campsite, Jud tried to see who and how many people he might be up against, but he could see nothing, not even a horse.

Jud dismounted and ground-tethered his own animal before pulling out the '73 Winchester from its saddle scabbard. He cocked the weapon and strode forward as stealthily as he could manage.

Then stopped abruptly.

From behind him, he thought, the sound of a horse: metal on rock and hard ground, the sound magnified in the near-silent darkness.

'Damnation!' he oathed under his breath,

'Which goddamn idiot boy is that?'

Crouching low, Jud watched and waited.

At the same moment, both Jack and Jefferson had tethered their mounts and were now only twenty feet away on either side of the campsite.

From his position, Jack could quite plainly see the body of a man lying near the blazing campfire. He cocked his rifle.

The dull metallic click brought Casey out of a deep sleep.

He didn't move, not sure whether the sound was real or imagined. But the sound of the approaching horse was not imagined, of that he was certain.

Silently, he reached for his rifle and dragged it towards him; better to be safe than sorry he thought.

The thick layer of cloud that had masked the thin silver light of the moon, chose that time to part.

Jud could just make out the outline of the approaching rider: skirt billowing, hat bouncing loosely behind the figure as the watery light of the moon silhouetted it.

The rider slowed to a walk, then halted.

'Hello the camp!'

Casey sat bolt upright.

'Sandy?'

Jud grinned.

The girl was obviously not on her guard. Jud was crouched less than ten feet away from her. He stood.

'Nice an' quiet, li'l lady. Nice an' quiet.'

Sandy was too shocked to make any noise, Jud grabbed the reins and roughly pulled her to the ground.

'Now you jus' do as I say an' everythin' will be OK,' Jud whispered to the girl.

'What do you want?' was all she could manage.

'Hush now, let's git moving.'

Gripping her upper arm tightly, Jud pushed Sandy towards the camp-fire.

'Sandy, that you?' The voice echoed through the air.

'Answer him, girl!' Jud stabbed the barrel of his rifle into Sandy's side.

She shrieked in pain and all but fainted.

Casey, aware that something was wrong, jumped to his feet. Jud had a perfect view of the man as he was backlit by the fire, rifle at the ready.

'Toss the rifle!' Jud yelled.

At that instant, a flash to his left erupted in a sharp crack as a weapon was fired.

Jefferson, seeing the man for the first time, aimed and shot.

The slug caught Casey high in the chest, spinning him backwards and into the blazing fire.

Both Jack and Jefferson rushed in.

'What the hell!' Jud roared as he saw his sons run into the campsite.

'Hell, Pa,' Jefferson said. 'I thought he was gonna shoot!'

'Next time *you* think'll be the first,' Jud said as he dragged the girl towards the waiting men.

This time, Sandy did faint.

Jud let her fall to the floor as the three men stood watching the burning man.

Casey was all but dead with a .44 slug in his chest, but the burning of his own flesh had brought him round. Struggling, with arms and legs on fire, he tried to get out of the flames, but he had no strength left in him. He could smell the sickly sweet stench of his own flesh, and the last sight he had before his eyeballs popped was of the skin on his left hand melting and dripping into the fire.

'Hot diggedy-dog!' Jefferson grinned. 'Look at him burn!'

Jud and Jack stared in fascination at the blackened, burning body, that writhed in the flames.

'Hell,' Jud mouthed, 'he must be dead now! But darned if he ain't still a-movin'!'

The movement stopped.

Jack, standing downwind, got the full blast of the thick smoke as it drifted lazily in the night sky.

Coughing, he threw up where he stood, his stomach retching as he threw up over his Levis and boots.

*

Sharper reined in quickly.

The single shot sounded like a distant canon exploding, shattering the still night air.

He was out of the sight now of the distant fire, but Sharper was certain that that's where the shot had come from.

Could be a cougar the man was shooting at, or a bear, he thought. But a single shot?

Thoughts crashed through his head like an avalanche. Why would anyone need to camp out so close to a town? Unless they were waiting for sun-up before riding in. But why wait?

Sharper decided to get the Bar B as quickly as possible now; he had to make sure the Henry gang were holed out there; then he'd check out the campsite before riding back to town.

He hardly needed to urge King on, the animal seemed to have a sixth sense, and leapt forward as Sharper's knees squeezed into his flanks.

It took thirty minutes of hard riding to reach the ranch.

It was dark: not a light shone. Sharper reined in and dismounted some fifty feet from the ranch house.

The open ground in front of the house was his biggest danger, if there was anyone inside, they could pick him off easy.

Then Sharper caught sight of a body lying just beyond the ranch house veranda.

Pulling out his rifle, he edged towards the barns to his left. At least there was cover there. King stayed where he was.

Barely breathing, Sharper crept around the barn, keeping his eyes fixed on the ranch house. Picking up a stone, he hurled it on to the veranda. The stone skidded across the boards and slammed into the side of the house.

Nothing stirred.

Keeping his rifle level, Sharper moved forward. The house was now twenty feet away; twenty feet of open ground.

As he'd done so many times before, Sharper formed a mental picture of his next action: saw himself running across the ground and reaching the veranda, he could almost see each footstep, and saw himself crouched low by the steps that led up to the front door.

He moved fast.

Skidding to a dusty halt at the foot of the steps, he waited a few seconds.

Still utter silence.

He mounted the steps in one leap and, using his

left foot, kicked the front door open. It wasn't locked and the staccato splintering of wood sounded like distant gunfire.

The house was empty. Sharper was sure of that now. But the smell!

He moved down the hallway towards the rear of the house, opened a door and stepped into the kitchen. Then he saw where the smell emanated from.

The room was thick with flies, which rose as one as he entered. Holding his breath, Sharper opened up windows and the back door, before tying his bandanna round his mouth and nose.

He didn't recognize the man on the floor, but he sure as hell hadn't died from natural causes. Blood, dry now and caked, covered the man's head. Worse, his head seemed to be alive. It moved just beneath the skin.

Sharper left the room by the back door, fighting the bile that rose into his mouth.

Gulping fresh air, he whistled for King, mounted and set off back to town.

Now he knew the Henrys were out on the loose and gunning for him.

ELEVEN

The cloying smell of cooked meat brought Sandy back to her senses. Her side throbbed and instinctively she tried to feel it.

He hands were tied in front of her. Her ankles were held together with a foul-looking bandanna.

Then full horror of what she had witnessed returned; her uncle, dead, burning on the fire and *she was breathing him in*!

Despite the gag she retched, choking, she coughed loudly.

Jud looked at her and grinned. He had plans for that little lady, just as soon as he got rid of the pesky stranger. Then the town and the ranch would be his. Yes sir, he thought, the high times are a-coming.

It was Jack who went to Sandy's side and released the gag. Spluttering and spitting, Sandy almost said thanks, but her throat was constricted and sore and all she wanted was to spit in his face.

'What now, Pa?' Jefferson asked.

'Reckon we ride into town, boys,' Jud replied. 'Got me a score to settle.'

'An' her?' Jefferson pointed to Sandy.

'Well, son o' mine, that's the clever bit, see. We got ourselves what's known as a hostage. This li'l lady here is kinda sweet on that there stranger. And now we got 'er, there ain't no need to go lookin' fer him! He'll sure as hell come looking for us!'

Jud laughed, thin lips spread over brown and blackened stumps of what were once teeth. His tongue licked those cruel lips as he stared at the girl.

'Then, boys, I'm gonna have me some funnin' with this li'l lady. Yes siree!'

'Aww, Pa! Can I have some of 'er too?' Jefferson licked his lips.

'We'll see, if'n there's anything left, boy, you can have it!' Jud grinned, flexing his fingers as he laughed again.

Sandy just hoped it would be over quickly.

'Come on, boys, saddle up, let's git movin'!'

Jack and Jefferson lifted Sandy into the saddle, and Jefferson kept the reins as he mounted his own horse and the party set off for town.

*

Maisie woke from a trouble sleep. Her ears strained to hear any noise, but the harder she listened, the more silent the house.

She got out of bed, reached for her dressing-gown and slipped her feet into her well-worn sheepskin slippers.

A chill ran down her spine and she shivered, even as sweat beaded on her upper lip. The air was hot inside the bedroom; having closed and locked the windows, the atmosphere was thick and cloying.

But something was wrong. She felt it in her bones.

Opening the bedroom door she stepped silently out on to the landing. She listened again.

Nothing.

Gripping the handrail, she descended the stairs, missing out the third from bottom as it creaked loud enough to wake a dead man.

Dead man!

Another shiver ran down Maisie's back.

Silently, she opened the door to Ben's room and peered inside.

His snoring and snorting told her that he, at least, was all right.

Then she went along the hall to the room Sandy occupied.

She turned the handle and edged the door

open, wincing as the metal hinges grated as loud as thunder in her ears.

She took a step inside the room, and, even in the darkness, knew it was empty.

She grabbed the oil-lamp and lit it with shaking fingers.

'Ben! Ben! She's gone!'

There was a coughing and spluttering from the next room as Ben came out of a deep sleep.

'Wha—?'

Maisie burst into his room like a great white bull, oil-lamp swinging as she held it high.

'It's Sandy. She's not in her room!'

Ben sat up awkwardly and rubbed his eyes. He looked around the room. 'Well, she sure as hell ain't in here!'

'I know that, you danged ol' fool! But where is she?'

'Have you checked *every* room?'

'No I ain't, I know she ain't here!'

'Sharper back yet?' Ben asked.

'If'n he was, do you think I'd be here shootin' the breeze with you?'

'Jumpin' Jehosephat! You don't think she's—'

Ben didn't finish the question.

'Sure as eggs is eggs,' Maisie replied. 'I'm a-goin' for the doc. He'll know what to do.'

Without waiting for a reply, Maisie left Ben's room.

'You better get some decent clothes on, Maisie,' he called after her. ' 'Less you wanna scare the man to death!'

But Maisie was already unlocking the front door.

*

The ride into town was slow, as the three-man Henry gang were hampered by having to lead Sandy's horse.

Bound and gagged as she was, Sandy could do nothing.

Her mind was in whirl: she knew Sharper was out at the Bar B which meant that the town would be at the mercy of the Henry gang.

Ben Robson, still bedridden, could be of no help, and the doc, good as his intentions might be, was no shooter.

Sandy racked her brain for inspiration.

But there was nothing she could do.

*

Sharper knew he had to get back to town – and fast. All thoughts of checking out the campsite vanished from his thoughts.

He knew the town was now undefended and his only hope was that the rooming-house was as solid a structure as it looked, and that Maisie, Sandy and Robson, hopefully aided by Doc Holliday, could hold off the gang long enough for him to throw in his two cents' worth.

King raced ahead following the almost invisible trail.

Sharper had complete confidence in his mount and kept his eyes fixed on the horizon, hoping against hope that just maybe the Henry gang were in no hurry and that he could catch them before they reached town.

He saw nothing.

Once more the high-flying clouds closed in on the moon and deeper and darker shadows flitted across the landscape.

In the distance, Sharper caught the faint howl of a coyote as the moon disappeared. Then near silence. The only sound came from King's breathing and the thudding of his hoofs along the hard-packed trail.

*

'Doc! Doc! Get your butt out here!' Maisie yelled, her face pressed hard against the glass-panelled front door.

'*Doc!*'

She heard footsteps first, then saw the dim glow of an oil-lamp being lit and watched as it

descended the stairs at the far end of the hallway;
the light not being bright, it seemed to be moving
of its own accord.

'Goddamn! Hold your horses, I'm a-comin' .'

Maisie waited impatiently as bolts and locks
were freed and Doc Holliday stood in his striped
nightshirt, holding the lamp high, staring into
Maisie's face.

'You got any idea what time it is?' Holliday
demanded.

'Nope. I ain't got a clue,' Maisie replied, grab-
bing hold of his arm. 'Sandy's gone.'

'Gone? Gone where?'

'How in tarnation do I know?' Maisie snapped.
'She ain't in her room's all I know, an' Ben's there
on his own.'

'Sharper not back yet?' Holliday asked, already
knowing the answer.

'You damn fool, you think I'd be here if'n he
was?'

'OK, let me dress an' I'll—'

Holliday stopped.

Just at that moment, the clouds parted once
more and the trail out of town was backlit with
the silvery-grey shards of moonlight.

In the distance, like spectres, Doc Holliday saw
the outline of riders. He couldn't make out how
many, but it was more than two, and if it was
more than two, it couldn't be Sharper. Which to

Doc Holliday, meant only one thing: the Henry gang.

Maisie followed his open-mouth gaze, but by this time the light had changed again and all she saw was darkness.

'What's wrong, Doc?'

'Riders. Yonder on the trail.'

'How many?'

'More'n one!'

'Come on, Doc, forget dressin'. Let's move!' Maisie grabbed his arm again.

'Hold your fire, Maisie,' Holliday said. 'Let me get my guns.'

'Just hurry, Doc, we ain't got much time.'

Maisie paced around the small veranda while Doc Holliday grabbed a Winchester and a box of shells and strapped on an ancient Peacemaker that he kept more for sentimental reasons than use.

'Right,' Holliday said. 'Let's go.'

If anyone had been peeking through draped windows at that time, they would have seen a sight fit to bust their breeches.

Maisie, built like a five-foot-high warhorse, was wearing a nightdress of white cotton that made her ample frame seem twice as large as she teetered down Main Street toting an old Henry rifle that was nearly as long as she was tall.

The doc, in his striped nightshirt, looked equally ridiculous with a gunbelt strapped to his waist, a Winchester resting on one shoulder and a flickering oil-lamp in his left hand, as he tried to keep up with Maisie.

When they reached the rooming-house, Maisie locked and bolted the front door.

'That you, Maisie?' a voice called out.

'Dang fool,' Maisie mouthed. 'Course it's me. Who you expectin'?'

Doc Holliday went into Ben's room. 'You got a gun, Ben?' he asked.

'Sure, soon as Maisie gets it for me. What do I need a gun for?'

'I think the Henry gang is riding into town, and Sharper's still out on the range. Sandy not back?'

'Hell no, I ain't seen hide nor hair of her.'

'Maisie, give Ben his guns back,' Holliday ordered.

'Just as long as he hits what he's a-shootin' at,' Maisie said.

'You jus' git my guns,' Robson said, 'and cut the sassy talk.'

Ben Robson turned to Holliday: 'Doc, can you shift my bed around a-ways? That way I can cover the window and the door.'

'OK, hang on.'

The heavy brass bedstead proved harder to move than either man thought, until Maisie lent a hand and Ben Robson was almost thrown to the floor.

'Dang hell-fire, Maisie! Careful, got a wound

here,' Ben yelled as he gripped the mattress to stop himself falling out of the bed.

'Sure packs a punch for a little 'un,' Doc grinned.

Maisie handed Ben his weapons. 'Jus' don't point 'em at me,' she said to the bedridden man. And there was no smile on her face as she said it.

'Hmm,' Ben replied.

*

Jud held up a hand.

'What's up, Pa?' Jefferson asked.

'Nothin' is up, boy,' Jud replied. 'There's the town.'

'What we gonna do?' Jack asked.

Jud spat into the ground, wiped a hand across his face, and sighed.

'Jeeze!' Jud said exasperatedly. 'I don't know, maybe breakfast?'

'Sounds swell to me,' Jack said, grinning.

'Boy, you ain't got no more brains now than you had the sorry day you wus born! We're gunnin' for that stranger, remember? The fella who kilt your brother?'

Jack's grin faded. 'So we ain't eatin' br—'

Jud drew his Colt and cocked the hammer back. 'Give me strength! So help me God I'll blow your damn head off one o' these days!'

'Hell, Pa, I didn' mean nothin' by it,' Jack pleaded. 'I jus' thought, seein' as how we were here an' all—'

'Shut your mouth, boy!'

Jud dismounted and manhandled Sandy to the ground.

'Now, I'm only gonna ask this once, so you'd best answer me, girl,' Jud said to Sandy.

His face was no more than two inches from hers and the stench of his body, his clothes, his breath, made Sandy almost sick.

She nodded.

'Now, I'm gonna take out this here gag, an' see this here pistola?' Jud drew his gun again and cocked the hammer once more.

'This is gonna be aimed at one o' them pretty legs o' yourn. See. I don't aim to kill ya none, least-ways, not 'til I had me some funnin'.' Jud leered into Sandy's face.

As she watched, his left hand came up to her mouth. The dirty fingers, cracked and blackened fingernails, reached into her mouth and roughly pulled out the filthy bandanna.

Sandy gulped in a lungful of fresh air. Her lips and tongue were as dry as a bone and she coughed as Jud's stench filled her nostrils.

'Wat – water,' she said.

'Sure, sure,' Jud said grinning once more. 'Jack, canteen.'

Jack dismounted, unhitched his canteen and strolled across to his pa.

Jud pulled the plug with his teeth, put the canteen to his lips and drank. When he'd finished he belched loudly into Sandy's face and his leering lips parted as he spat a mouthful of water into her face.

'That enough for ya?' He grinned.

Despite herself, Sandy's tongue flickered once across her lips.

'Now,' Jud moved on. 'Where's that fella holed up?'

Sandy coughed again, and tried to clear her throat, it still felt as though half the bandanna was lodged in it.

Jud pressed the barrel of his pistol into her left thigh – hard.

'He's – he was – in the rooming-house,' Sandy croaked.

'An' where might that be?' Jud asked. He moved the barrel of the Colt closer to Sandy's crotch, and dragged an evil-looking tongue across his cracked lips.

'It – it's opposite, the – the saloon,' she stammered.

Jud moved the pistol barrel up and down her crotch for a few seconds and then back to her thigh.

'An' who else might be in there?' he asked.

Sandy coughed. The smell of Jud Henry was cloying. She'd never thought a human being could smell so badly. But then, she thought, calling him *human* was paying him a compliment; calling him an animal was an insult to all animals.

'As far as I know, only Maisie and Ben.' She turned her head so as not to breath in the fetid breath coming from Jud's mouth.

Jud gripped her upper arm, she could feel his fingers digging into her flesh through the thin material of her dress.

Jud leaned even closer. His nose was almost touching hers.

'You sure do smell sweet, li'l lady,' he breathed into her face.

Sandy couldn't help herself. She gagged, bile rising into her throat. She couldn't turn her head away, with Jud's grip on her arm and his face so close; she was sick down his stained leather vest.

'Goddamn!' Jud yelled. Both Jack and Jefferson held back laughs.

'You damn bitch!'

Jud reholstered his Colt and swung his left arm out and slapped Sandy hard across the side of her face. She staggered, but Jud's grip on her arm held her upright. Blood ran from the corner of her mouth, and stars danced around Jud's head as she looked at him, her eyes small and intense.

'Got some spunk,' Jud said. 'I'll give you that, li'l

lady.' He let go of her arm and Sandy sank to the floor, legs and arms still bound tightly. She couldn't get up. Her head swam, and there was little feeling in her arms and feet.

Jud got down on one knee and whispered into Sandy's ear: 'Gonna have me a fun time with you, gal. That's for damn sure!' He spat by the side of her face.

Sandy stared at the ground watching the thick, almost black glob of tobacco spit slowly sink into the sand.

She closed her eyes and thought *if I'm gonna die, I hope it's quick.*

She turned her head defiantly and stared hard into the black eyes of Jud Henry.

His lips were parted into that leering grin again, but his eyes looked like the gateway to hell.

For what seemed like long time, the two stared at each other: Sandy in fear and loathing, Jud in eager anticipation of what he was going to do with her after he'd killed the stranger.

'I never thought to ask,' he said, sounding almost human. 'What the hell is that stranger's name anyways? I plumb forgot.'

'Wade,' Sandy whispered, more of a mental plea than an answer to Jud's question.

'Say what? Speak, li'l lady, I can't seem to hear ya.'

'Wade,' Sandy repeated, louder this time.

'Sharper Wade!'

Jud got to his feet, belched again.

'Get her saddled,' Jud said to Jack, 'an' let's get this over with.'

Jack, aided by Jefferson, picked Sandy up as if she were a sack of beans, forced the foul gag back into her mouth and laid her across the saddle once more, loop-tying her so she wouldn't slip off.

'Wade, huh? Sharper Wade!' Jud mouthed, and the grin reappeared.

TWELVE

As Sharper crested a rise, he reined in King. Wiping the horse's neck, he felt the sweat damp on his fingers and patted King affectionately.

'Good boy, King,' he said aloud. 'Soon be there, then you can rest up on them oats.'

The horse snorted once, and bobbed his head, convincing Sharper he understood every word.

In the distance, Sharper could just make out a dim glow.

The town.

Still, he thought, he hadn't even asked the name of the place. He'd ridden in the night before, only twenty-four hours ago, and yet it seemed as if he'd been there a whole lot longer.

He studied the town and the approaching trail from the east. From this distance, given the poor light, he could see very little.

Reaching into his saddle-bags, Sharper pulled out his old army-issue spyglass. The brass tube gleamed dully in the watery moonlight. Removing the caps, he peered through the now extended telescope at the small town.

He moved from dim light to dim light, but saw no movement, no sign of life at all, in fact. If he was surprised, he didn't show it.

He lowered the telescope and gazed at the sky. Thick clouds still obscured the moon.

Looking through the telescope again, he moved his sighting from west to east, slowing, trying to pick up the main trail. There were places where long shadows appeared to be moving, others where the darkness was impenetrable.

Then he caught movement.

Or at least, he thought he did.

Scanning back quickly, Sharper moved the telescope slowly from right to left.

Yes. Riders.

Too dark to count, but more than one.

The Henry gang hadn't reached town yet. Good.

He closed the telescope, replaced the end-caps, and stowed it away.

Sharper wished he knew more about the terrain. The land outside the township was virtually unknown to him. The only trails he'd used had been the one from the west when he'd ridden in, and the one to the east where he'd ridden out to the Bar B.

From his vantage point, the easiest route was a

straight-line ride into town. But trails were laid out in times gone by for a reason. Sometimes the easiest route turned out to be the most dangerous.

Patting King's neck once more Sharper mouthed: 'Come on boy, not long now.'

Trusting his mount's surefootedness, Sharper gave him his head. Cautiously, King edged down the slope off-trail. Sharper had made up his mind to take the straight-line ride to town.

Skirting yucca, cactus and sagebrush, King wound his way further down the slope; the ground was softer here, and King's hoofs were sinking into the running sand, making progress slower.

At last, the flat bed of the valley was reached and Sharper had to rely on a mental note of the direction he needed to take.

He rode on.

*

Jud Henry could see no point in rushing. Leading the way, he walked his animal to the outskirts of town and halted.

His black eyes scanned Main, moving from building to building down one side, and then back up the other.

'Leave the horses here,' he ordered.

The three men dismounted, ground-tethering their animals. Jack and Jefferson checked their rifles, then their six-guns, before joining Jud.

'What we gonna do with her?' Jack asked.

'Bring her with us, you dang fool!' Jud replied.

Jack untied the lariat securing Sandy to the saddle and lowered her to the ground.

Her feet were numb and as they touched the ground she grunted through the gag and fell.

'Loosen her feet,' Jud called across to Jack.

'Hell, Pa, she could run!'

Jud spat into the ground and lifted his face to the sky as if seeking divine help.

'Jus' do it!' he said softly, too softly, Jack thought. He kneeled down in front of Sandy and untied the rope around her legs.

Sandy gasped as blood throbbed through her feet and, without waiting, Jack manhandled her upright.

She fell again.

'Give her a minute,' Jud spoke softly again. He spoke as though he were talking to a child. And Sandy realized that that was exactly what he *was* doing.

Jack drew his Colt and stood by Sandy.

'Put the gun away,' Jud said.

'But, Pa—'

Jud turned and, even in the darkness, his eyes bore into Jack's. 'I said, put the gun away! Now!'

Jack swallowed hard, but did as he was told.

'Right, now, you ready, li'l lady?' he asked

Sandy.

She nodded silently.

'Then let's be movin',' Jud said and he led the way straight down the middle of Main Street.

*

Maisie was in the upstairs front bedroom, the Henry resting on the windowsill. She had a perfect view of Main; from left to right she could see the whole town.

She swallowed hard as she recognized the big man walking towards the rooming-house.

'*Jesus!*' she said, then crossed herself and apologized to God for taking his son's name in vain.

Lifting her bulk from the small chair she occupied she all but ran downstairs.

'They're here,' she called softly to Holliday and Ben.

'How many?' Ben asked.

'I only seed the one,' Maisie replied.

Holliday moved first, he ran up the stairs, not making a sound. He entered the front room and peered through the window-pane.

To his left, not more than a hundred yards away, he could see Jud Henry. Behind him, he saw—

'Holy Mother of God!' he mouthed. 'They got Sandy!' He ran to the doorway and shouted again, 'they got Sandy!'

Jud halted. He heard the yell but not the words.

His face creased as his gaze lit upon the rooming-house, then swept to his left to the saloon.

He moved the Winchester from his right hand to his left, and took out his Colt.

'Wait there,' he told Jack and Jefferson.

He strode forward, Colt at the ready, and stood outside the rooming-house.

'Wade! You in there?'

Silence.

'Sharper Wade! I'm callin' you out!'

Still silence.

Jud Henry pointed his Colt at a downstairs window and gently eased the trigger back.

The slug shattered the window and embedded itself in the wall behind Ben Robson's bed.

'Wade! You there?'

Inside the rooming-house, the doc turned to Ben and Maisie.

'What in hell do we do now?'

'We wait,' Maisie said. 'Sharper'll return. So we wait.'

A second bullet winged in through the upper pane of the front room. This time the slug hit the ceiling lamp, shattering the opaque glass.

'Goddamn!' oathed Ben.

'We can't just wait!' Doc Holliday said.

'You got any better suggestions?' Maisie asked.

Moving forward, the doc stood by the side of the shattered window.

'This is Doc Holliday,' he called out. 'Sharper Wade isn't here.'

Everyone ducked down again as a third slug ripped through an upstairs window.

'You wouldn't be lyin' to me now, would ya, Doc?' Jud Henry called back.

'No, siree,' the doc replied. 'Sharper rode out to the Bar B to check it out for Ben Robson here.'

'Robson there, is he?' Jud said.

'Sure am, Mr Henry,' Ben called out. 'Got myself shot up pretty bad in the leg. That's how come I never came back to the ranch.'

'Well, that sure is a shame, there, Mr Robson,' Jud drawled. 'Seems like one o' my boys got hisself kilt. You wouldn't know anythin' 'bout that, I guess?'

'We heard it, Mr Henry,' Robson said. 'Your boy shot down three men, killed two, then took on Sharper.'

'So I hears,' Jud said, then fired another shot at the rooming-house.

'Got me a purty gal out here,' Jud added. 'Seems like a shame to have to hurt her some.'

'You send her in here right now,' Maisie yelled.

'Can't do that ma'am,' Jud said. 'Reckon we'll wait over to the saloon. Don't none o' you try anythin'. Jack and Jefferson here'll be coverin' ya.'

Turning, Jud beckoned to Jefferson. His son walked slowly through the ankle-deep dust of Main and stood before his father.

'Git round the back, boy, an' make sure none o' them git out.'

Jefferson shrugged, he knew there was no point in arguing with his pa. While he was stuck out back, they were going to be sitting in the saloon, more than likely sampling the whiskey.

Jefferson spat and turned on his heel.

'We got the back covered too,' Jud called out to the rooming-house. 'So you folks jus' sit tight and maybe, jus' maybe, you'll be fine an' dandy.'

Jud had no intention of anyone being fine and dandy. Not the doc, not Ben Robson, and certainly not Sharper Wade.

Jud turned his back on the rooming-house and waved for Jack to bring Sandy with him. The three crossed the street and climbed the steps to the boardwalk and entered the saloon.

If only Doc Holliday had been standing in front of, instead of beside the shattered window, it could have all ended there.

*

Sharper reined in quickly. The shot cut through the air, shattering the silence.

He was less than a mile away.

'Come on, boy, let's go.' Sharper dug a heel into King's side and they galloped forward.

In less than two minutes, Sharper was on the west side of Main. He dismounted, tethered King, patting his neck in gratitude.

Taking out his Winchester, Sharper checked it was fully loaded, and, satisfied that it was, he moved into the shadows.

Sharper crept forward, then halted as an oil-lamp flickered into life in the saloon.

Looking across the street, he could just make out the shattered windows of the rooming-house.

Sandy! he thought and for the first time in a long while, Sharper felt a strange feeling in his chest.

He shrugged it off. Getting sentimental would-n't help him now, he thought.

He had a job to do.

The rooming-house was in complete darkness, but as he stared hard, he saw one of the down-stairs drapes twitch. It twitched again, and this time was drawn back an inch or two.

He couldn't make out who was there, but he knew it was the room they'd put Ben Robson in. And as Ben was bedridden, it must be someone else.

Sharper thought quickly.

He reached into his vest pocket and brought out a vesta and cracked it on his thumb nail. Using his right hand to shield it from the saloon side of the street, he let the match burn awhiles, hoping that whoever was peering from the window would see it.

The match burned out, and Sharper tossed it to the ground, thinking: they either know I'm here or they don't!

Why the hell don't they get out of there? Sharper wondered. Then it dawned on him.

If the Henry gang were in the saloon, someone must be at the rear of the rooming-house. He almost cursed at his own stupidity.

He moved back towards King, then silently crossed the street and ducked down an alley between the general store and an empty office.

When he reached the rear of the buildings, Sharper rested on his haunches then, working back to the rear of the rooming-house, studied the terrain.

Just as he thought. His gaze rested on a battered Stetson, beneath which showed the soft red glow of a cigarette. As he watched, the glow brightened, as the man sucked in, then dulled and disappeared.

Sharper was no more than feet away.

Edging out further, he got behind the man and, placing his Winchester on the ground, took out his hunting knife.

With the knife between his teeth, he homed in.

Jefferson sighed loudly. All he could think of was that he was hungry and he was thirsty. Worse, he was fed up.

He pulled out a ready-made from his vest pocket and struck a light.

The flame never reached the cigarette.

Soundlessly, the blade sliced through his neck.

The cigarette between Jefferson's lips fell slowly to the ground as his eyes opened wider than they had in years.

Turning, blood pouring from his neck, he looked at the man who was crouched behind him.

His lips moved, frothy blood oozed out of his mouth and ran down his chin to join the torrent that spurted from his neck.

In less than two seconds, Jefferson knew he was dying.

A gurgle escaped his mouth as his right hand went for his gun which was resting on his lap.

Still looking Sharper, almost sightlessly, in the eyes, Jefferson managed to squeeze the trigger.

*

Jud stopped abruptly, glass half-way to his cracked lips.

The sound of the shot puzzled him. Was it that dang fool kid out back? he wondered. Darn it if he hadn't told him not to do any shooting.

Jack's eyes were everywhere at once, checking the batwings and the windows either side, his gun already in his hand.

Sandy's eyes brightened. Could Sharper be back? Or was it from the rooming-house?

*

Doc Holliday had seen the flare of the match.

He couldn't make out the face of the man who struck it but, with the Henrys in the saloon, and one round back, it must have been someone else.

Sharper!

The name jumped into his brain and he smiled.

'What you grinnin' at?' Maisie asked. 'I cain't see nothin' here to grin at, you darn fool.'

'Nothin', maybe, Maisie. Or somethin',' Holliday replied. He stood up and left the front room to find the kitchen.

Once there, he peered out of a window.

Sure enough, he could the man out in the yard, the fool was even smoking!

As he watched, Holliday's attention was drawn to another dark figure creeping up behind the guard.

It was him. It was Sharper!

It took less than a minute for Sharper to dispose of the smoking man, but the shot came as a surprise.

The slug winged through the window, narrowly missing Holliday, and shattered a plate that hung on the wall.

'I'll be damned!' Holliday said as Maisie rushed into the room.

'It's Sharper,' Holliday said. 'He just killed another Henry.'

Maisie unlocked the back door, but before she could leave, Holliday grabbed her arm. 'Get back to Ben,' he said, 'I'll give Sharper what help he needs.'

Jefferson Henry was still sitting bolt upright; the life had left him only moments ago as Doc Holliday drew to Sharper's side.

'Knew you'd make it back,' Holliday breathed. 'Jud and the other son are in the saloon, waitin' on you.'

Holliday paused, then, in a softer voice added: 'Sharper, they got Sandy.'

'*Got* her? You mean she's—'

'No, no, Doc interrupted. 'They got her in the saloon. Guess she went out ridin' after you and they—'

'She all right?' Wade asked.

'Far as I could see,' he replied. 'How you want to handle this?'

Sharper now addressed himself to the saloon.

'With Sandy bein' in there, I can hardly go in guns blazin',' he said, then paused, deep in thought.

'Seems like I'll have to call him out,' he said at last.

'But there's two of 'em,' Holliday said.

'I know, maybe you can cover my back. You get back into the house, send Maisie upstairs and take the downstairs window. Keep your eyes peeled on the saloon windows and batwings. I'll call Jud out, but you can bet your life, his son'll try and get a bead on me.'

'Sounds risky, Sharper,' the doc said.

'Them Henrys could kill Sandy any minute. I don't trust 'em any more than you do, but we can't afford to wait 'em out.' Sharper had made his mind up.

'Good luck, son,' Holliday said. 'Give me five minutes to get set. We'll do our best.'

'Thanks, Doc, I know.'

The two men shook hands as if it would be their last meeting. As Holliday stood, the dead body of Jefferson Henry fell sideways. Holliday swallowed – hard.

Without waiting, Sharper moved back to retrieve his Winchester. Then, making sure no Henry had come to investigate the shooting, he made his way back to Main.

Halting by the side of the rooming-house, he waited, giving the doc and Maisie long enough to get in position.

He waited exactly five minutes.

Standing, he leant the Winchester against the wall of the house, tightened the cinch of his Stetson, adjusted his cross-over gun belts and stepped out on to Main Street.

*

'Get her over here!' Jud ordered.

Jack cut through the ropes that held Sandy in the chair and dragged her roughly to the front of the saloon.

'What you reckon, Pa?' Jack asked.

'I reckon Jefferson's bin a mite careless, is what I reckon.'

'What're we gonna do?'

'Stop your damn fool questions, boy,' Jud said. 'I'm gonna do what I set out to do: kill that damn Sharper Wade fella, have me some funnin', and git me a ranch.'

'You don't think it would be—'

'Boy, you ain't never thought, don' try it on now! Now shut the hell up an' let me think!'

Jack held Sandy's arm so tight she could feel the bruises coming.

'You cover her,' Jud finally said. 'I'm goin' out.'

Before Jud could move, a loud, deep voice penetrated the air.

'Jud Henry!'

Jud put a finger to his lips and whispered: 'Get a sightin' on him boy.'

Jack was a mite flustered as he still had Sandy with him. Pushing her roughly to the floor by the saloon window, he placed a booted foot on her rump. 'You make one move, lady, an' I'll blow your damn head off!'

Jud walked towards the batwings, a smile flickered across his lips. His plans, his dreams, were about to be fulfilled. he didn't give a damn about John, or Jefferson, good riddance he thought, he just needed to get rid of the one person who could ruin his retirement.

Sharper Wade.

Pausing to one side of the batwings, Jud checked his six-gun: loaded. He glanced to his right where Jack, rifle ready and the girl pinned beneath him, was also ready. Jud gave him the thumbs-up signal.

Jack, for the first time in his life, winked at his father.

Jud replaced his Colt and stepped towards the batwings, slowly easing them open.

Directly ahead of him, on the far side of the street, stood his nemesis: Sharper Wade.

'We done got your sweetheart in here, Wade!' Jud called out.

'She ain't *my* sweetheart,' Sharper replied, his voice as cold as steel.

Jud swallowed involuntarily. That was not the response he'd expected.

Slowly, he licked his lips, glancing once more to his right, and stepped out on to the boardwalk.

Sharper had not missed the sideways glance, and allowed himself a brief glimpse of the far saloon window.

Although the lamplight was low, he caught the reflected light off a gun barrel. He just hoped Maisie or the doc were checking out the windows and not staring at Jud Henry.

Sharper had already decided on his move; he knew the other Henry boy was beading him right now. His only hope was to get Jud Henry to draw, dive to his left and, simultaneously, draw both pistols: one for Jud, the other for the window, or rather, just below it.

It was a long shot, but Sharper knew better than to rely, no matter how well-meaning they were, on Maisie and Doc Holliday. He had to act as if he were alone.

And Sharper Wade had never felt more alone in his life.

Jud took another half-pace forward. Sharper knew what he was trying to do: get him to concentrate on him, and ignore anything else. A wry grin parted Sharper's lips.

'I'm ready,' Sharper said.

Jud Henry's opinion of himself as a shootist was a tad higher than actuality.

Sharper watched intently as the man's body seemed to change as, instead of a swift, smooth arm action, Jud Henry crouched and drew. But he was slow, far too slow.

Unsighted, Jack could only see Sharper, so he had no idea that gunplay had started until the crack of Jud Henry's Colt snapped.

Jack pulled the trigger of the Winchester, and by pulling it, lost all aim.

At the same instant, Sharper dived left and forward, a Colt in each hand emitting smoke and flame and death.

Jud Henry, down on one knee, was knocked back into the saloon as the slug caught him in the chest.

Jack Henry gazed at his crotch, dropped the rifle and screamed. Blood coursing down his legs, he collapsed as the slug shattered his pelvis. Sandy felt the warm moisture splatter on her face as Jack collapsed, writhing in agony. It would take

Jack a long time to die. But die he would.

Sharper stayed low in the dirt. Behind him, belatedly, came two rifle shots that flew towards the saloon. There was no answering fire.

Another shot from behind, before Sharper called out, 'Hold fire!'

Cautiously, Sharper arose from the dirt on to one knee, both Colts levelled and cocked. He could see Jud. Jud was still. He could hear Jack.

Sharper stood up, crossed the street and entered the saloon.

Jack was still screaming at the top of his voice; it was an eerie sound, a death sound.

On the floor, beneath the now shattered window and clapboard, was Sandy, bound, gagged, and covered in blood.

'Oh God!' Sharper holstered his weapons, moved Jack's kicking body to one side without paying him much heed, and knelt by Sandy.

Gently he raised her head and removed the gag.

She gulped. Sharper grinned.

Taking out his own bandanna, he wiped her bloodied face, looking for any sign of injury.

'It's – it's not my blood,' she managed to say, looking towards the screaming Jack.

Sharper lifted her into his arms and left the saloon, walking back towards the rooming-house. Doc Holliday and Maisie were already outside, their rifles at the ready.

'You can put them away now,' Sharper said.

'Sandy! Oh, Sandy,' Maisie said, and threw the cocked rifle to the boardwalk.

It fired, narrowly missing Doc Holliday as the bullet sped harmlessly into the night sky.

'Jesus!' the doc said and near fainted.

'She's OK, Maisie, she's OK,' Sharper said.

Slowly, those who were left of the townsfolk came out on to Main Street, before ambling over to the saloon.

Jack had stopped screaming now, he moaned silently, death was taking him over.

Jud had died instantly, and the townsfolk stepped over his body, making for the bar.

Sharper placed Sandy on her bed and called for a bowl of water, to clean the blood from her face.

Maisie brought it in and, tenderly, more tenderly than Sharper thought he was capable of, he wiped the filth from her face.

He dried her off, then leant forward.

Their lips met briefly for the first time, just as Doc Holliday barged into the room.

'Well, they're all dead now!' he said gleefully. 'Oh, er, sorry, I didn't, er, well, guess I'll just, er, well, thought you folks'd like to know, is all.' The doc retreated from the room backwards, hitting the doorframe with his elbow as he left.

'Guess that's all sorted then,' Sharper said and stood up.

'Guess so,' Sandy said, and smiled.

Then it was Maisie's turn to enter the room unbidden.

'Grub'll be up in thirty minutes,' she said, 'an' I ain't runnin' no cheap house! You two git washed up an' presentable, else you'll be out in the livery!'

'Yes ma'am – Maisie,' Sharper said.

Sandy smiled up at him, and Sharper felt he might stay on awhiles.